black box

ALSO BY JULIE SCHUMACHER

Grass Angel

The Chain Letter

The Book of One Hundred Truths

black box

a novel by
julie schumacher

Delacorte Press

Published by Delacorte Press
an imprint of Random House Children's Books
a division of Random House, Inc.
New York

Delacorte Press and colophon are registered trademarks of Random House, Inc.

Visit us on the Web! www.randomhouse.com/teens

Educators and librarians, for a variety of teaching tools, visit us at
www.randomhouse.com/teachers

LIBRARY OF CONGRESS CATALOGING-IN-PUBLICATION DATA
Schumacher, Julie.
  Black box / Julie Schumacher. — 1st ed.
    p. cm.
  Summary: When her sixteen-year old sister is hospitalized for depression and her parents want to keep it a secret, fourteen-year-old Elena tries to cope with her own anxiety and feelings of guilt that she is determined to conceal from outsiders.
  ISBN 978-0-385-73542-1 (hardcover) — ISBN 978-0-385-90523-7 (Gibraltar lib. bdg.)
  [1. Depression, Mental—Fiction. 2. Sisters—Fiction. 3. Family problems—Fiction.
4. Interpersonal relations—Fiction. 5. High schools—Fiction. 6. Schools—Fiction.] I. Title.
PZ7.S3914Bl 2008
[Fic]—dc22
                                    2007045774

The text of this book is set in 13-point Fournier.
Book design by Trish Parcell
Printed in the United States of America
10 9 8 7 6 5 4 3 2 1
First Edition

With eternal gratitude:
Thrace Soryn, Carol Melie Seabrook, and Melissa Bank

This book is for Paul Cody

1

We can hear someone screaming as soon as we get off the elevator. At first it's hard to tell what the person is saying—the sound swells and fades, a high-pitched moving ribbon of noise—but as we walk down the narrow hallway (my mother reaches for my hand), I can hear the word *"Out"* and then *"Out of here"* and then *"Let me out."*

We hang up our coats and lock my mother's purse and my father's keys in a metal locker. The screaming rises and falls. My mother glances at my father, and I can tell what she's thinking. *We should have left Elena at home.*

We have to walk through a metal detector. The button on my jeans sets it off with a beep, and a security guard with a sagging belly gestures toward me and waves a wand up and down in front of my stomach. "Any knives?" he asks.

"What?" My brain is numb because of the screaming. *"Letmeoutletmeoutletmego."* It fills the hall and seems to suck up the air all around us.

"Do you have any knives?" the guard asks. "Anything sharp? Corkscrews, Swiss Army knives, nail files, knitting needles, razor blades, paper clips, scissors?" He looks tired. The bags under his eyes match the bag of his belly.

"Not with me," I say stupidly, as if admitting that I have left my knife-and-scissor collection downstairs in the lobby.

"All right, go ahead, then."

The screaming continues.

We come to a door with a small window in it. The thick, heavy glass in the window is crosshatched with wire.

My father presses a button, like a doorbell, on the wall.

"Can I help you?" A crackling voice emerges from the intercom.

"For Dora Lindt," my mother says, leaning forward on her tiptoes and speaking into the metal box by the doorbell. "We're her family. Her parents and her sister."

Through the narrow window in the door I can see two men partly dragging and partly carrying a screaming person toward us. It's a tall skinny girl dressed in gray pajama bottoms and a dark green T-shirt, and she is flailing with all her might, hurling her body back and forth, her long wheat-colored hair whipping one of the men, who is probably twice her size, across the face.

My mother and father and I all stare at her, as if watching some terrible new reality-TV show.

"Oh my god," my mother says.

The screaming girl lifts her head and looks toward the window and meets my gaze. Her eyes are green and unfocused. Her face is a mask.

"She almost looks like Dora," I say.

And then my mother falls down in the hallway beside me, and the screaming girl on the other side of the glass is dragged into a room by the two men, who quickly lock her away.

2

How did my sister fall through a hole in her life and into some other life below?

I'm not sure how it happened. Sometimes I still have trouble believing that it happened at all.

3

It was a regular afternoon after school in September. Dora was at the kitchen table, dipping crackers into milk. She was the only person I knew who liked soggy crackers.

"You're going to have to clear off the table soon," my mother said. "And put that box of crackers away. I'm making dinner."

Dora kept dipping. Up, down, up. Another wet cracker.

"We're having spaghetti," my mother said.

I picked up my books and put them in my backpack.

"Have you both finished your homework?" my mother asked. The school year had just started. I was in ninth grade and Dora was in eleventh. We were in high school together for the first time.

"Not yet," I said. "I still have Spanish. I have to conjugate *los verbos*."

"What about you, Dora? Do you have homework?"

My sister shrugged in slow motion. She was almost five foot ten and bony; I used to tell her she looked like a praying mantis.

"Your grades weren't very good last year," my mother said. "You have so much potential. You need to apply yourself and get organized. What did you do with that calendar I bought you?" Like me, my mother was the sort of person who enjoyed making lists and then crossing things off them.

Dora didn't answer. I had seen the calendar on the floor of her bedroom, most of the dates blacked out with pen.

"You'll want to start thinking about college soon," my mother said. "Instead of moping around the house, you should join a club or go out for a—"

"Don't," Dora said. She opened her fingers like a hinge and let go of the cracker, which slid to the bottom of her glass.

My mother put a pot of water on the stove. I could tell she was getting annoyed but was trying not to show it. "Sometimes I wish I could get inside that head of yours and find out what you're thinking." She paused and looked more carefully at Dora. "You haven't brushed your hair," she said. "You used to keep your hair so neat."

"I wish I was dead," said Dora.

Dora already had a therapist, a person my mother had started sending her to in the summer, after she got fired from a babysitting job: she'd turned on the water in the tub and plugged the drain, then taken the kids for a walk to the playground.

Now, because my mother claimed it was "a good idea in times of stress," we were all going to have therapists. My parents shared one. So that I wouldn't feel left out, I got one too.

Mine was an older woman with short white hair like a cap on her head. I thought she looked like someone's grandma. When my mother left me at the office door with her ("I'll be in the waiting room, Lena, if you need me"), I almost expected her to offer me a hug or a cookie.

She closed the door. We sat down. We each had an armchair and a small side table. Her table had a clock on it. Mine had a clock, a plant, a jar of stones, and a box of tissues.

The Grandma Therapist said she was glad to meet me. Then she made a speech about confidentiality. Everything I said that didn't involve endangering my own life or somebody else's would be kept in the strictest confidence. During our sessions I could say anything I liked. She hoped I would trust her. She put her hands on her knees and waited.

I looked at the rug on the wooden floor between us. It was one of those homey coiled types supposedly woven from rags. *Someone should have warned this woman about me*, I thought. I wasn't much of a talker. My mother liked to call me "reserved." Dora said that socially, I had the skills of a three-horned toad.

"I don't know what we're supposed to be doing here," I said when the therapist finished with her speech.

She spread out her hands as if to show me what they looked like. "We talk. That's it. You tell me what you're thinking and what you're experiencing. Your mother told me you might want to talk about your sister."

"Oh." I still wasn't sure what I was supposed to say. Dora was Dora. She was a slob and I was neat. She was emotional and fun; I was more straightforward. That was the way we had always been—the way things fit and felt right between us.

Eventually the Grandma Therapist made another short speech, at the end of which we agreed that it was probably hard to be the younger sister of a person who was depressed. "Did it come on suddenly?" she asked, her white hair catching the light from the window. "Or did you see signs?"

What would the signs have been? I wondered. Dora had always been unpredictable and goofy and moody. She could fit eight large marshmallows into her mouth and still sing "The Star-Spangled Banner." She could write with both hands at the same time, signing her own name backward and forward. Once, at our grandparents' cabin, she had tried to tie me with strips of cloth to the underside of a bunk bed, so that when our cousin climbed in to go to sleep, I could drool on his head.

If there had been signs of something changing in Dora, I hadn't seen them.

The Grandma Therapist leaned forward in her chair. "Depression is an illness, and no fault of the person who suffers from it. Sometimes there are causes we can point to, and sometimes there seems to be no cause at all."

We looked at each other.

"Are there any concerns that I can address for you?" she asked. "Do you ever worry that because your sister suffers from depression, you might suffer from it someday too?"

"No." I knew I wasn't like Dora. I wasn't affected by the things that affected her. It was as if, growing up, Dora had occupied a certain space and developed a certain kind of personality, and I had taken what was left over. On a barometer, Dora was a storm on the horizon; I was the needle that always pointed to *steady*.

"There's no real reason you *should* worry," the Grandma Therapist said. "Though there is a genetic component. Depression can run in families."

Run, I thought, was not the right word for what was happening inside Dora. Ever since that afternoon in the kitchen, the clockwork within her seemed to have stopped. One day she was arguing with me about whose turn it was to use the hair dryer, and the next day (or was it the next week?) she was wrapped in a blanket on the floor of her room, picking at her hangnails and refusing to talk.

Looking down at the coiled rug at our feet, I remembered a game Dora and I used to play when we were little. She called it Lifeguard, and it involved Dora being a drowning victim on the living room floor. She would launch herself off the couch and onto the rug and flail around as if disappearing into the sea-blue carpet. I was always the lifeguard. I was supposed to stay on the couch and throw her a rope (we used ribbon or string), which Dora struggled to tie around her waist. If she couldn't tie it (if, for example, the water was cold and her hands were numb), I was allowed to leap off the couch and drag her to safety, the two of us scrabbling toward the tile floor in the hallway (Dora was always gasping for breath), until one of our parents saw us thrashing around on the carpet with a mess of string and told us we would have to play outside. For a year or two, Lifeguard was our favorite game.

"You're smiling," the Grandma Therapist said. "What are you thinking?"

"Nothing. I was just thinking about Dora. That Dora's going to be okay," I said.

"So you're an optimist."

"No. I just know she's going to be okay."

The Grandma Therapist pressed her lips together.

I didn't care what she thought. She didn't know Dora the way I did. I knew that Dora always came back again, no matter how deep the water, and no matter how hard her fall.

5

Dora got worse.

6

Maybe, I thought, she shouldn't have told us how bad she felt. Maybe once those words were out of her mouth they gave her permission to fall apart. She stopped doing her homework. She lost weight. She fell asleep on the couch in the middle of the day but wandered around the house in the middle of the night, wearing a long-sleeved black T-shirt and underwear and a pair of old socks. Whenever my parents talked about what she was going through, they said she was "down."

I thought about *Alice in Wonderland* and the rabbit hole.

Dora pulled at the skin around her nails and made it bleed.

"Why are you doing that?" I asked her.

"Doing what?"

I pointed at her nails. A drop of her blood ended up on my finger.

She wiped it off. "I don't know. Would you hand me my pills?"

I gave her the little brown bottle that lived by the toaster—an antidepressant. Dora swallowed a pill every morning and every night before she went to bed.

She unscrewed the childproof cap while I watched. "Every family needs a problem child," she said, tossing back a pill by jerking her pointed chin into the air. "You should probably thank me. I've saved you from taking on that role."

"Thanks," I said.

"You're very welcome, Sister Elena." Dora had a

collection of names for me: Elvin, Elward, Lay-Lay, Layton, Sister E, and El-Dora. She linked her arm through mine. Dora was rowdy and theatrical where I was private, tall while I was short. Her hair was long and almost blond while my dark hair barely touched my shoulders. But we had always been close. We were like right and left hands laced tight together.

"Adoradora," I said. My nickname for her.

She twisted the cap back onto the bottle. "Life sucks," she said.

"Sometimes it does," I agreed. "But sometimes it doesn't."

"You're such a compromiser." She slumped against the kitchen counter.

"Okay," I agreed again. "I guess I am."

7

My parents' therapist must have told them to be more parental. They came home from their sessions armed with pamphlets and books on parenting. They went around the house inventing rules. Dora and I weren't going to be allowed to sleep late on weekends. There would be no more "lingering" in our bedrooms; we were supposed to find "productive uses" for our time.

My mother in particular liked to enforce this new set of rules. She was always telling Dora to get off the couch. "I don't want you sitting there watching TV all day," she said.

But Dora wasn't watching TV. She was sitting on the couch not doing anything. I was keeping her company, sitting beside her.

"Mom's turning into a real nag," I said.

Dora rearranged her long legs underneath her.

"Maybe she's hitting—what do you call it?—the change of life," I said.

"She already went through it." Dora's voice was dull and without expression; all the shine had gone out of it.

"Really?" Dora always seemed to know about things that went on around the house. "So she can't have kids anymore," I said.

Dora slowly rotated her head on the stem of her neck and said she would thank me not to remind her that our parents slept in the same bed and probably still, on occasion, had sex.

"Oh," I said. "Right."

We sat on the couch and watched Mr. Peebles, our ancient tabby, arrange himself into an orange coil on his favorite chair. He glared at us for a minute, then went to sleep.

"How many kids do you want to have?" I asked. "I mean, when you're older."

"None." Dora twisted her hair into a sort of haystack at the back of her head. Some of her fingers were circled with Band-Aids; the rest were a mess.

"Why none?" When we were younger, Dora and I used to plan out our future families. Dora had always wanted two girls and a boy, and I wanted twins. We'd imagine what our kids were going to look like and then we'd argue about what we should name them. Dora always came up with unusual names: Thibald and Sidra and Fabrienne.

"Because kids are a pain. They just mess up your life," Dora said, erasing in a couple of sentences my future nieces and nephews. "Besides, there are too many people in the world already. The earth is too crowded."

"Oh." I imagined people fighting for space at the edges of continents, some of them losing their footing and falling into the sea. "Maybe we could adopt."

She didn't answer.

I turned up the volume on the TV and switched to the Spanish-language channel. My teacher suggested that everyone watch it, but I could barely understand a word.

Dora was poking at the back of her hand with a paper clip. "Do you hate school as much as I do, Elvin?" she asked.

"You don't hate school," I told her.

"Why don't I?"

"Because you have friends there," I said. "And you like to learn things."

On TV, a woman held up a package of diapers and said something incomprehensible.

"You should try to remember when you're sad what it's like to be happy. You just have to remember." I took the paper clip away from her. "Everything's going to be okay. This is just a phase you're going through. Pretty soon you'll feel better."

Dora rested her head on my shoulder. "You're really annoying sometimes, Lena," she said.

8

Toward the end of September, on a cloudy Friday afternoon after school, Dora swallowed a handful of antidepressants. She was only supposed to take two a day, but she took a lot more. I was up in my room when my mother found her in the kitchen, swallowing one small oval pill after another with a glass of juice. My mother started shouting Dora's name. I ran downstairs in time to see her trying to count what was left in the bottle, but her hands were shaking and the little tablets rained down on the floor.

We drove Dora to the hospital. I sat in the backseat beside her. For some reason I had brought my schoolbooks. Dora closed her eyes and slept. Traffic was terrible.

"Elena. Keep her awake," my mother said.

So I pinched Dora. Hard, above her elbow. It felt good to do it.

"Ow," she said. "Jerk." She opened her eyes and grinned at me. I didn't think she was trying to kill herself. Why would a person who was trying to kill herself smile at her sister?

"She's okay, Mom," I said. "It must have been a mistake."

My mother started to cry.

9

I didn't cry; I wasn't a crier.

I didn't cry in fifth grade when our cat, Mr. Peebles, got hit by a car. And in seventh grade, when I had an enormous splinter dug out of the bottom of my foot, I didn't flinch. "Unrufflable," my father called me.

I thought about the episode with the splinter while we waited in the emergency room, Dora chewing on her hands in the chair beside me and my mother around the corner, sobbing into her phone. Across from us, a man with his arm wrapped in a bloody towel sat next to a woman with a sleeping baby wrapped in a blanket. "Look how tiny that baby is," I said to Dora. Only two hours earlier I had been at school, trying to understand how my new graphing calculator worked.

Eventually a nurse called Dora's name. A doctor interviewed her by herself in a room down the hall. He came back fifteen minutes later (the man with the bloody towel had been called to an examining room, but the woman with the baby was still waiting) and said that Dora hadn't done herself any serious damage and didn't need *medical* treatment; but he was going to admit her for a few days. They had a room upstairs.

"Upstairs *where?*" my mother asked, as if the hospital were a maze and the doctor intended to lead Dora into the distant heart of it.

When my father showed up a few minutes later, clutching

his briefcase and looking confused, my parents left me in the waiting room by myself. I understood that it was my job to remain very calm. I remembered that during the episode with the splinter, Dora had held my hand and put her forehead close to mine and made me look at her, away from the doctor with his tray of instruments, even while the bottom of my foot was on fire.

"I'm right here for you. Right here. You're amazing, Lay-Lay," she had said.

And, because my sister had said it, I was.

10

The reason people went to the hospital when they were depressed, my parents explained that night, as if I were six instead of fourteen, is so they'd be safe. Dora needed a safe environment. Once she felt secure again, and more like her old self, we would bring her home.

"How long will that be?" I looked at the pizza we had ordered for dinner, which no one had touched.

"Not very long," my father said. He had an ink spot on his shirt from keeping a pen in his pocket. He glanced at my mother. "The important thing—for Dora—is that we try not to overreact."

The hardest moment at the hospital, I thought, had come right before Dora went upstairs. We had followed a nurse through a series of hallways to an elevator, at which point Dora had to take off her silver hoop earrings and her three silver rings and then her sixteen silver bracelets—one for every year she had been alive—and hand them to my mother. She did it slowly, the bracelets clinking in my mother's palm. Dora was never without her bracelets; seeing her take them off, one after the other, was almost like watching her undress.

My father pushed the pizza box toward me. "We should eat. Lena, are you hungry?"

The phone rang. We let the answering machine pick up. "Hey, Dora, why aren't you answering your cell? It's Kate. We thought you were coming over at seven-thirty. Get your nutty self over here, *fast*." We heard people laughing in the background. The machine beeped its goodbye.

"They'll take good care of her at the hospital," my father said. "And we'll see her tomorrow."

My mother was wiping up an invisible stain on the table.

I took a slice of pizza from the box. Someone had to eat it.

"She's going to be fine," my father said.

"I know that," I answered.

We didn't see Dora the next day—Saturday—because that was the day when the two attendants shut her in a room and locked the door.

My father and the security guard helped my mother up.

"I'm fine," she said, holding her elbow. "Just ring the bell."

My father rang it and asked to speak to one of the nurses. We waited. Eventually a nurse named Ralph (according to his name tag) walked very slowly to the door as if he were wading through invisible water. He pressed the small round button on his side of the door and told us through the intercom that we would have to come back another time. In order to receive visitors, Ralph said, all patients, according to the adolescent psych ward rules, had to be *compliant. Compliant* meant physically and emotionally willing to follow procedure and—

My father tried to interrupt. "She was admitted yesterday afternoon. She just got here. Her name is Dora Lindt. We only want to know that she's—"

But Ralph hadn't stopped talking—maybe the intercom was stuck or only worked in one direction. We could ask to meet with a social worker, Ralph continued in a droning voice, but as far as visiting, that wouldn't be possible until Dora stopped arguing with the staff and learned to follow procedure.

My parents and I stared at him through the narrow window.

This kind of thing happened sometimes, Ralph said. It wasn't unusual and was probably best considered a period of adjustment. The first few days were often difficult. He removed his finger from the intercom button. Then, oddly, he said something else, his lips moving silently. Finally he tapped the glass twice with his finger and walked away.

12

My mother spent the rest of the day in bed with a headache. My father spent it moving his collection of tools around on the pegboard walls in the garage. He was thin and restless, like Dora; neither one of them was very good at sitting still. Every now and then he came in from his pointless rearranging to check on me. "Do you have any homework?"

"You already asked me that," I said.

"And what was your answer?"

"That I don't do homework on Saturday. I always do it on Sunday."

"That's right," my father said. "Now I remember." He sat down next to me on the couch and we thumb-wrestled twice; he beat me both times. After he pinned me the second time he pinched my chin and told me I was turning out to be a decent kid. "Love you," he said.

"Thanks, Dad."

"I wasn't finished." He spread out his arms above his head. "Love you like this: as big as the sky." My father was corny. He liked corny phrases.

He stood up and stretched. "We've just got to be patient," he said. "That's all there is to it. It's going to take time but she'll come out of this with flying colors. You won't watch TV all day, will you?"

"Probably not," I said.

"Good girl."

Finally he went back to the garage and I watched a couple of animal shows and about an hour of the Spanish channel.

That night my father set four plates on the kitchen table, then remembered that Dora wasn't home and had to take one away.

13

On Sunday right after breakfast we went back to the hospital. We walked through a sudden rain to the double doors of the main entrance, then shook the water from our clothes and crossed through the emergency room waiting area, where people with dislocated arms or broken fingers—things that were probably easy to fix—waited their turns the way we had done two days before.

My mother pushed the button for the elevator and turned to me as if discovering my existence for the first time. "Are you sure you're up for this?" My mother was short, like me, and I worried I would grow up to be a lot like her: determined, chubby, and a pain in the neck. "That was traumatic yesterday," she said. "You can wait in the lobby if you don't want to come."

"Of course she wants to come." My father put his hand on my shoulder.

I felt like their private puppet. *Let* me *make her talk!*

The elevator opened. Everyone else who filed in with us was carrying flowers and GET WELL! balloons. A little girl was dressed as if she were going to a birthday party.

We got off on the fourth floor (no one else got off with us) and nodded to the security guard.

"Let's not say anything to upset her," my mother said. "We'll just be ourselves."

Who else would we be? I wondered.

We stowed our jackets in a locker, walked through the metal detector, and buzzed the bell by the door.

I had brought Dora's favorite pajama pants and a sweat-shirt that said IOWA SURF CLUB, but the nurse who answered the door and let us in said Dora couldn't have them because the sweatshirt had a hood on it and the pants had a string. "No ropes, no strings. And nothing sharp," the nurse said. "I'll keep these behind the desk so you can take them home."

Beyond the desk where the nurses worked, I saw a group of kids—maybe a dozen of them—sitting in gray plastic chairs in a semicircle. One girl was asleep sitting up. The others didn't seem to be doing anything. A boy lifted his head and stared at me blankly, and I thought of the animals at the zoo, living their lives behind glass while a series of spectators either ignored them or hoped they would get up and do something worthwhile.

The nurse—her name tag identified her as Bev—said that Sunday mornings weren't technically set up for "socializ-ing," but since we hadn't been able to see Dora yet, she sup-posed we might stay for a short visit.

"Where is she?" My mother hugged her arms to her chest.

One of the kids—he had short blond hair and what ap-peared to be fifteen or twenty stitches in his forehead—pointed toward a set of open doorways on the right: "She's in her room."

My sister's new bedroom, like every other bedroom on the adolescent psychiatric ward at Lorning Memorial Hospital, had two narrow beds, both of them bolted to the vinyl floor, two wooden cubbies bolted to the wall, a gray smeared win-dow that didn't open, and a bathroom door that didn't lock.

She was reading a comic book on the bed nearer the win-dow, her long legs straddling the mattress. She was wearing jeans and a hospital gown. The gown was printed with teddy bears holding stethoscopes.

"Dora," my father said. "Hey. It's great to see you."

My sister turned toward us where we were clustered in the doorway. There was something different about her, I thought. There was something new about the way she looked at us, as if we weren't the family she had expected.

I thought my mother was going to cry again; instead, she rushed forward. "We tried to visit you yesterday but you were . . . upset." She sat down on the bed next to Dora and touched the side of her face, her arms, her hair. "You look good, sweetheart."

Dora put down her comic book. Her skin was blotchy and her hair was braided. Dora never wore braids. "They locked me up," she said. "I wasn't 'upset.' I was throwing a fit. They wanted me to eat something disgusting and when I wouldn't eat it they decided I was anorexic."

My father told her that throwing a fit was probably a bad idea and that she might want to maintain an even keel.

One of the nurses from the desk poked her head through the doorway, seemed to count us, and nodded.

"Ten-minute checks." Dora picked at her fingers. "Someone sticks their head in here and stares at me every ten minutes, even at night." She tugged on the hem of my T-shirt. "What do you think, Lena? Nice place, huh?"

"Great," I said. "It's really elegant."

Dora's expression changed slowly; she almost grinned. "Let me show you around." She swung her leg over the bed and stood up. "Closet," she said, pointing with a flourish at the wooden cubbies. "For all those up-to-date hospital fashions. And look in the bathroom: no hooks. And no shower rod. They don't want you to hang yourself. I can't even hang up my towel."

My father was standing in front of the window, facing out, even though there was nothing but a parking lot to look at.

"No blinds on the windows," Dora said, still posing like a game-show hostess. "No shoelaces, no razors, no scissors or pencils. No cell phones. No music."

I was waiting for her to say that she didn't need to be there; I was waiting for my parents to tell her it was time to come home.

"I know this is hard," my mother said. "Just do what the doctors and the nurses tell you. We're supposed to meet with the doctor on Wednesday."

"Why aren't we meeting with the doctor until Wednesday?" my father asked without turning around.

"Because," my mother said. Her voice was taut. "That's when they told us we could get an appointment."

Dora sat down on the bed again. She flopped face-first against the sheets and let my mother scratch her back. Dora loved to be scratched. "I wanted more clothes," she mumbled. "I thought you would bring some."

"We'll bring them next time," my mother said.

"And I want my hairbrush." Dora's eyes were closed. "And I want underwear and socks and a pile of T-shirts. And some gum and a book. I need something to read."

"Your father's writing this down," my mother said.

My father searched for a pen.

"And bring me a sandwich?" Dora asked. "The food here is terrible."

My mother kept scratching, her fingers tracing a circle on Dora's back. What kind of sandwich and what kind of bread? she wanted to know. Would mayonnaise or mustard taste better with turkey?

We tried to talk normally for a while. Dora said the kid

with the stitches in his head had been hospitalized three times and knew some of the people who went to our high school. The nurses were mean to him, she said. Some were mean to her also. Most of the day, she said, the patients sat around doing nothing; they had nothing to do.

Another nurse poked her head through the door: "We need to ask you to wrap things up."

"I'm like a bug under a freaking microscope in here," Dora said. She reminded my mother about the sandwich.

We stood up. My mother hugged Dora; my father kissed her.

"Little El. What the heck are you doing over there?" Dora asked.

I walked toward her and she reeled me in and held on to me tightly, her bony arms a collar around my neck. "Do me a favor?" she asked, with her mouth by my ear.

"Sure," I said. "Name it."

"Save me," she said.

14

In the car on the way home, my father talked about how great it had been to see Dora. He said he felt better now, having seen her and having been in her room. He said the nurses seemed attentive. My mother stared out the window. I thought about Dora asking me to save her. She wasn't serious, I thought. What was I supposed to save her from?

When we got off the highway my mother turned around in the front seat and said she assumed I understood that Dora's "situation" was confidential. Obviously, she said, I would have to be very, very discreet. There were very few people at school, for instance, who would need to know.

"I'm sure Lena understands that," my father said.

I did understand. "But you're talking about an American high school," I said. "Everyone in the building probably already knows."

"We're going to tell her guidance counselor and the nurse, but that's it," my father said. "They'll keep it quiet."

"Sure," I said, remembering the kid with the head full of stitches.

My mother gave me a look.

At school Monday morning, the first two people I ran into (I didn't know either one of them) said they felt bad about my sister, and how long did I think she would be locked up? The third person asked me what it was like on the crazy ward.

I went to my locker to get my books. In math—a subject I ordinarily liked and did well in—we took a quiz, but I only answered about half of the questions. In English we were reading *Hamlet* out loud, and I had to read about Ophelia losing her mind.

In history I put my head down on my desk. I just wanted to think for a few minutes but I ended up falling asleep. Someone tapped me on the shoulder. I thought it would be Mr. Clearwater. He'd been Dora's teacher in ninth grade too. ("Giant handlebar mustache," she had warned me, rolling her eyes. "He wants all the kids to think he's a biker.")

But it wasn't Mr. Clearwater. It was Jimmy Zenk, who lived down the street from me but who I'd probably spoken to about twice in my life. Jimmy had failed at least one grade and seemed to be getting through high school on his own special schedule. Recently he had shaved a stripe through his hair so his head looked like a lawn that someone had just started mowing. "Hey. Lena. Elena Lindt." He was sitting behind me, poking my neck with a pencil eraser. "I heard about your sister."

I lifted my head off the desk and wiped a ribbon of spit from my cheek. "I didn't think you knew my name."

"Yeah," Jimmy said. "I know it. I know a lot."

I rubbed my eyes and watched Mr. Clearwater hunt through his desk for a piece of chalk.

Jimmy poked at my neck again.

I waited for him to come out with some kind of weird I-shaved-my-own-head-person remark.

"Is she at Lorning?" he asked.

I nodded. There was only one other hospital near where we lived, and it was mostly for veterans.

"What does she think of it?"

I decided not to answer. Mr. Clearwater had found his chalk and was busy writing on the board.

"I know someone who was there once," Jimmy said. "That's why I'm asking. Lorning's okay for car accidents, or maybe for having your appendix out, but the psych ward has a lot of problems."

"What kind of problems?"

Mr. Clearwater snapped his fingers at us. The pointed tips of his mustache, Dora had explained to me, were waxed.

"Meet me on the bus," Jimmy said, waving to Mr. Clearwater and not even bothering to lower his voice. "I'll tell you then."

15

I almost didn't make it to the bus because my locker was stuck and I had to kick it open. When I finally got my books and ran out of the building and found bus #20 in the lineup, I saw that Jimmy Zenk was sitting at the back with a bunch of guys in black T-shirts. I didn't know them. Dora and I had gone to a nearby private school through the eighth grade (Creative Learning Academy), so we were both considered freaks and hopeless cases when we got to high school. Me in particular. "Don't expect to have any friends for a while," Dora had warned me. "There's no welcome committee." She was right. It was nearly October and, so far, most of the people who acknowledged me in the halls were my sister's friends.

We rode past the strip mall and the grocery store and turned left at the park, the bus chugging its way through a tangle of suburbs. Northern Maryland—the part where we lived—was full of suburbs with names like Babbling Creek and Willow Run and Soaring Eagle Estates. Most of the houses were alike except that some had porches (like ours) and some had an extra-large garage. I lived in Sheffield Oaks, but I wasn't sure what an oak tree looked like.

Jimmy Zenk got off at the second-to-last stop and so did I. I studied him for a minute. His jeans had a hole in them, down one leg, fifteen or twenty inches long, and down the arm of his long-sleeved T-shirt in ballpoint pen someone had written LOST CAUSE. "Hey," I said. "Did you forget your backpack?" The bus was disappearing around a corner.

"No. I don't have one," Jimmy said. He wasn't carrying any books.

"What do you do with your homework?"

"I do it at school. Or I just bring home what I need. The necessaries, you know?" He pulled a wad of folded paper and a pen from his pants pocket. "Less than ten percent of homework is educational," he said. "I've seen the statistics."

We looked at each other. "So," I said.

Jimmy patted the shaved part in his hair and ran his fingers along the bristles. "I think I should cut this again," he said. "What do you think? Do you cut hair?"

"Not like that," I said. It was starting to rain.

"You think my hair's ugly?"

"I think you want it to be."

"Good answer. Clever." Jimmy tilted his head to look up, his Adam's apple sharp and pointed. "Do you remember my older brother?"

"Not really." I had a vague memory of an older Jimmy-like person who had dropped out or graduated and moved away a few years before.

"Mark," Jimmy said. "That's his name. Mark. Short for Marcus but no one but my father ever called him that, and we haven't seen my father for years, which is probably a good piece of luck all around." He looked at me as if I were a question he was hoping to answer. "Do you want to come to my house so you don't get wet? I could make us a snack."

"No, I don't think so." I started home. But then I turned around and saw that Jimmy was still standing behind me. "Did your brother Mark have to go to Lorning? I mean, to the psych ward?"

Jimmy held out his hands to catch the rain. "It's kind of a

long story," he said. Behind him, above the trees, a white sheet of lightning filled up the sky.

"Is your brother crazy?" I asked. "Or was he depressed?"

"Are those my only two choices?" Jimmy asked.

A car was approaching so we moved to the curb. The rain was coming down harder. "We just saw Dora yesterday," I said. "She's going to be fine."

Jimmy kicked at a clump of weeds growing out of the sidewalk.

"What?" I asked.

"Nothing. I'm just thinking you're probably afraid to be seen with me. You're probably thinking that talking to me is like committing social hara-kiri."

"Not really." I shook my head.

"Why not?"

"I don't really know anybody," I told him. "I don't hang out with people from school."

"Huh. Interesting," Jimmy said. "So you've got nothing to lose by coming to my house. Am I right?"

I had never been inside Jimmy Zenk's house, even though it was only a couple of blocks away from mine. Because the outside was dull and ordinary (garage on the right, tree on the left), I expected it to be dull on the inside, but it wasn't. It was bright and artistic, with oversized abstract paintings on the walls.

We went into the kitchen. Jimmy opened the refrigerator. "Do you want something to eat? You want some chocolate? Some soda? Cigarettes?"

"No, I'm not hungry. And I don't smoke."

"I don't either. Just trying to be polite. You know—the full range of offerings." Jimmy was opening and closing cabinets.

I looked around. The walls were a bright cobalt blue, and instead of a table and chairs the kitchen had a booth, like in a diner. The booth had silvery vinyl seats and a black stone surface between them to eat on. I sat down. "So. What's the long story about your brother you were going to tell me?"

"Do you like chocolate soda?" Jimmy asked. "Chocolate's good for you. It lightens your mood."

I told him I didn't want anything, but he took two glasses from the cabinet and set them on the counter.

"Okay, Mark," he said. "It's a drugs-and-violence story, mostly. He was pretty destructive. He liked to hang out with people he shouldn't have. Bad judgment, you know? Then finally, a couple of years ago, he punched his hand through the door at a counselor's office and got arrested, and everything went downhill from there."

I remembered the kids I had seen at Lorning, staring at nothing in their plastic chairs. "Are most of the people on the psych ward—you know . . ."

"No. Are they what?"

"Violent like that. With a lot of problems. And messed up on drugs."

Jimmy poured powdered chocolate into the glasses, then added milk and club soda.

"I don't mean anything against your brother," I said. "But Dora wouldn't punch a hole in a door, and she's not destructive. She's just—" I remembered my parents' word. "*Down*. It's a totally different situation."

"Yeah." Jimmy held a glass toward me. His eyes were gray blue, the color of a lake. "Everyone's different. Taste this," he said.

I took a sip of the fizzy chocolate (it wasn't good, but it

wasn't bad, either) and tried to get used to the idea that I was actually having a conversation with Jimmy Zenk—Jimmy who had played in the sewer drains when we were little, Jimmy who wore black clothes every day of the week, who sat at the back of the bus with the local druggies, and who went to school but didn't own a backpack or carry any books. Inside my own backpack, the pencils and pens were in separate compartments, and the notebooks were organized according to color. "Did you fail ninth grade?" I asked.

"Some of it."

"So that's why you're taking ninth-grade history?"

"I'm making up for a couple of classes here and there. And I like Mr. Clearwater. He and I have an understanding." Jimmy drained his glass and carried it to the sink and washed it. "The problem with Lorning is that they like to lock people up," he said. "You probably haven't seen them, but they have these little isolation rooms. They're like padded cells."

I remembered Dora being locked away.

"That probably won't happen to your sister." Jimmy ran his hand along the stubbly path in his hair again. "But there are better places you could send her."

"She's not going to be there long," I said.

Jimmy shrugged. "Okay. But if your parents want some names of other places, let me know. My mom's got a whole list. She hated the doctors that worked at Lorning. Especially a guy named Siebald. Dr. Siebald is nuts."

I stood up. "My parents know what they're doing," I said. "But thanks for the soda."

"Sure. Whatever." Jimmy followed me to the door. "Here's my phone number." He gave me a white card with his name printed in red in the middle. J. ZENK, it said, with a number below.

"Why do you have business cards?" I asked. "Are you dealing drugs?"

"No. Do you think everyone who has a business card is dealing drugs?"

I stuffed the card in my pocket and picked up my backpack. "Just because your brother hated Lorning doesn't mean it's a terrible place."

"It wasn't only my brother," Jimmy said.

"Okay, and your mom. But—no offense—what would your mother know about hospitals?"

Jimmy opened the door. "My mom's a psychiatrist," he said.

16

We weren't allowed to see Dora on Monday, but on Tuesday before dinner we talked to her on the phone—using all three extensions—for several minutes.

"How was your day, Rabbit?" my father asked. Rabbit was one of the nicknames he had invented for Dora when she was little.

"It sucked," Dora said. Her voice sounded thick, as if she'd swallowed a mouthful of syrup. "Hang on a second."

"What's the matter?" my mother asked.

I could hear someone swearing.

"Somebody's flipping out in the hall behind me," Dora said. "A couple of the kids in here—they're certifiable. There's a guy across the hall who tried to burn down his house. With his parents in it. And also his dog. We gave him a hard time about the dog. Animal rights and all that."

"Did you see the doctor this morning?" my mother asked. "You had an appointment with him, didn't you?"

No answer.

"Dora?"

"What? Oh, he was late," Dora said. "Actually, he never showed up. So I worked on a puzzle."

"What else did you do?" my father asked.

"Hold on," Dora said. "*What?* I'm talking to my parents. *Yes*. I'm on the phone. I got permission."

"Sweetheart?" my mother asked.

There was a pause and an intake of breath; I knew Dora was getting ready to cry.

"Most people in the world are so freaking normal," she sobbed. "Everyone in the world is normal other than me."

"Well, I don't think—" my father began, but she cut him off.

"All day they keep asking me how I feel. That's all they do. They go around asking and asking and asking."

"What do you say to them?" I asked. "Do you tell them you're sad?"

"No." She took another deep breath. "It isn't like sadness."

"Then what is it like?"

Another pause.

"I can't describe it," Dora said. "I don't know how."

17

When the phone call was over, my parents and I sat down to dinner with Dora's place empty. Four chairs, three people.

"How was school today?" my mother asked.

"It was all right." We were eating take-out Chinese. No one had cooked or bought groceries for days.

"What's your favorite subject so far?" My father loaded up his plate.

"When is Dora coming home?" I asked.

My mother wiped her mouth on a napkin. "They haven't told us yet," she said.

I punched my fork through a mushroom, noticing that we had ordered all the dishes that Dora liked: *mu shu* chicken, asparagus with mushrooms, and deep-fried crab. She liked more adventurous food than I did. Once, when I wasn't paying attention, Dora had hung several crab claws around the rim of my drinking glass. "When will they tell us?"

"Soon," my mother said.

I folded some *mu shu* chicken into a Chinese pancake. "They ought to let us visit her," I said. "Everyone else who goes to the hospital is allowed to have visitors."

"This is different," my father said.

"How is it different?"

He wrinkled his forehead and got ready to answer, but my mother held up her hand and cut him off. She was obviously working up to a speech—something that in private she had already practiced. I took a bite of my pancake and let her talk.

She said Dora's "situation" was complicated. It wasn't as if she had a broken leg. Finding the right sort of drug and the right sort of treatment could take a while. But the important thing to remember was that Dora would get better. A lot of people suffered at one time or another from "the blues." It was fairly common. My father's uncle Bill, whom I'd never met and had barely heard of, had apparently once been depressed; but he had fully recovered. And so would Dora. We just had to be patient. She was getting the best of treatment.

"In fact," my father said, glancing at my mother as if to say, *I am sharing this tidbit of information with Elena,* "we're finally going to meet her psychiatrist tomorrow, at ten-fifteen. What was his name, Gail?"

"Siebald," my mother said. "Dr. Siebald." She picked up her chopsticks and told me not to worry. Everything was going to be all right.

18

Outside the nurse's office at school, there was a poster that asked, *Are You or Is Someone You Know Suffering from Depression?* Below the big print at the top was a kind of checklist.

- Do you have difficulty falling asleep?
- Do you sleep more than 12 hours in a 24-hour period?
- Do you feel sad more than half the time?
- Have you noticed a change in your eating habits?
- Do you have difficulty concentrating?
- Do you have low self-esteem?
- Do you think about suicide or death several times a week?
- Have you lost interest in your usual activities?
- Do you feel restless or anxious?

Six months earlier, I wouldn't have answered yes to any of those questions, if I'd been talking about Dora. Sometimes she was sad and sometimes she was restless; sometimes she slept for eleven hours. But Dora was quick. Dora was funny. Dora could play "Hot Cross Buns" on the piano with her feet.

"I never realized she was feeling that bad." Dora's friend Lila came up behind me so both of us were standing in front of the poster. "I can hardly believe it." Lila's hair was a black silk curtain.

"She'll be all right pretty soon," I said.

Lila waved to someone at the end of the hall. "Do you get to talk to her very much?"

"Not really," I said. "We're only allowed to visit twice a week. Thursday and Sunday. And it's family only."

"I know. I tried to call the hospital and talk to her yesterday but they wouldn't let me. I even said I was a doctor."

"You said you were a doctor?" I stared at Lila. She was vice president of the honor society.

"I'd do anything for Dora," Lila said. "Wouldn't you?"

That week at school, between classes, I did my best to avoid other people. I did homework at lunch. On the bus, I sat by the window and watched the strip malls give way to neighborhoods and vice versa. No one asked me about Dora. No one except Jimmy, who leaned toward me in Mr. Clearwater's class and tapped me on the shoulder. "Hey," he said. "So how's she doing? Is she doing okay?"

I nodded.

In case I had accidentally thrown the first one out, Jimmy gave me a second business card. "Call me whenever," he said. "I'm usually not doing very much."

"Mr. Zenk: please stop bothering that female student," Mr. Clearwater said.

"Yeah, okay. Her name is Elena," Jimmy said.

"I'm aware of her name; just leave her alone," Mr. Clearwater sighed.

A few minutes later Jimmy tapped me on the shoulder again and said that if I needed to find him, he'd be at the back of the bus on the way home from school.

Dora and I used to make fun of the way families on TV sit-coms were always sitting down for a heart-to-heart talk. *Son, your mother and I need to speak with you about something important,* one of the parents would say, and Dora would shriek and throw back her head and try to smother me with a pillow.

I used to be glad that our family didn't engage in these heart-to-hearts, that we didn't sit down to have Important Conversations.

But now I got the feeling that my parents were talking to each other without me, that Important Conversations were occurring when I wasn't around.

That Thursday night at six-thirty, I got my jacket out of the closet. Visiting hours at Lorning started at seven. "Ready?" I yelled.

My father was standing right behind me. "Ow." He covered his ears.

"Sorry," I said. "I didn't see you."

"Apparently not." He cleared his throat. "Elena."

"What?" The way he pronounced my name, enunciating all three of its syllables, made me understand that something had been decided.

"Your mother and I are going by ourselves tonight." My father looked at me for a minute, then squatted down to tie his shoes. On top of his head, right in the middle of his hair, he had a bald spot the size of a quarter. Once, when he was taking a nap, Dora had put a sticker there that said, IT'S MY BIRTHDAY!, and he'd worn it for hours without finding out. "We talked with some of the staff yesterday, and they think it makes better sense for us to visit privately for now."

"What do you mean, 'privately'?" I asked.

"You have homework to do anyway," my mother said, coming down the stairs. "You won't be doing Dora any good if you aren't keeping up in all your classes."

I felt uneasy, as if someone had run the tip of a feather up the back of my neck. "Is something going on?" I asked. "Did you meet her psychiatrist? Is he really weird?"

"Why would her psychiatrist be weird?" my mother asked.

"I don't know. Why can't I go see her?"

"I'm not going to stand here and argue with you," my mother said. "Write your sister a note. Write something supportive."

"You can go with us next time," my father said.

I grabbed a piece of paper and quickly scribbled *Dora—I miss you. Feel better. Lena.* Then I added a P.S. in code. Dora had invented the code when we were younger, and she had drilled me until both of us were good at it. The code involved replacing every letter of the first word in a sentence with a letter two places later in the alphabet, and every letter of the second word with a letter two spaces earlier. And so on. Back and forth.

I held the pen tightly in my hand and wrote, *Tgogodgt rfgq?* Which meant *Remember this?*

My father looked at his watch. "Almost finished?"

It had been a while since I'd written code. *Oqo ylb Fcf bgrafcb og,* I wrote. *Mom and Dad ditched me.*

"You know the rules," my mother said. "It's a school

night. Get your homework done. No socializing and no boys in the house while we aren't here. There are plenty of left-overs in the refrigerator you can eat for dinner. We'll be back in two hours."

I folded the note in half and creased it and handed it to my father.

"You're supposed to bring her a book," I said, noticing that my mother was holding a sandwich and a stack of clothes. I looked around on the shelf in the hall and found a book of fairy tales—Dora loved fairy tales—and gave it to my mother. Then I stood at the window and watched my parents drive away. If I was allowed to visit her next time, that meant Dora would be staying at Lorning for over a week.

I reached into the pocket of my jeans, found a crumpled white card with red writing, and picked up the phone. "Jimmy?"

21

Measure each angle in diagram 3A, recording your measurements below. Indicate whether the angle is acute or obtuse.

"_Obtuse_ means stupid," Jimmy said. He had come over right after I called him, walking in the front door without even knocking; but once he showed up I had second thoughts. I told him that my inviting him was against the rules, that he could only stay for half an hour and I was going to be doing homework the entire time.

"Thanks for the warm welcome," he'd said. Now he was leaning over my shoulder at the kitchen table, reading the questions on my math worksheet.

"How's she doing?" he asked. "How long has it been— almost a week now?"

"Six days," I said. On the inside of my backpack were six black checkmarks all in a row.

"Is she coming home soon?"

I didn't answer.

"Hard," Jimmy said. "That's really hard. Even if you pretend it doesn't bother you, it probably does. They like to hold on to people at Lorning. And they like to prescribe a lot of drugs." He tapped a finger against my worksheet. "You got the first two wrong, by the way." He stood up and stretched and opened the refrigerator. "You're supposed to offer me something to eat. You know, the whole hostess thing. Do you know how to cook?"

"Do I look like a housewife?" I erased my answers to the first two problems while Jimmy closed the refrigerator and ran his finger along my mother's cookbooks.

"Dr. Siebald's her doctor," I said.

Jimmy's finger stopped on *The Joy of Cooking*. "I'm thinking ramen," he said. "Or macaroni and cheese. Those are probably our best options. Do you want to put tuna in the mac and cheese?"

"Did you hear what I said? Siebald is the doctor you warned me about."

"I heard you." He took a pot from the cabinet and started filling it with water. "Finish your homework. I'll make the noodles."

I put my worksheet away and closed my books. "It could have just been that your mom didn't like him. I mean, didn't like Siebald," I said. "My parents met him and they think he's okay."

"I'm looking for cheese," Jimmy said. "And I mean real cheese. This orange powder that they give you in the box is radioactive." He opened the refrigerator again, found a block of cheddar, and started to chop it up with a knife.

"You aren't listening to me," I said. "And we have a grater."

"I am listening to you," Jimmy said. "I'm a very good listener. My hearing's been tested."

I gave him the grater.

"The confusing thing," he said, "is that whenever I ask you how she's doing, you say you aren't worried. But that doesn't make sense."

I watched him peel some mold from the cheese. "It's not like I don't worry at all," I said. "It's just—"

"Just what?"

I wasn't sure what to say. Why was I talking to Jimmy Zenk about Dora in the first place? "She's always been moody," I said. "And worrying doesn't do any good, does it?"

"Probably not," Jimmy said. "Do you want to work on this cheddar?"

A few minutes later I was opening a can of tuna and putting the noodles into boiling water. When I turned around to ask him something, Jimmy was gone. He came back holding an electric razor.

"Where did you get that?" I was draining the tuna into the sink, and the oil from the fish was all over my hands.

"Found it upstairs," Jimmy said. "I guess it's your dad's. Will he mind if I use it?"

When I didn't answer (what could I say?), Jimmy opened the door and went outside, stood in the middle of the back lawn in sight of the window, and shaved another stripe across his head, this one from just above his eyebrow to the nape of his neck. He blew the hairs out of the razor, shook his head like a dog, then waved to me at the window and came back in. "You should only have electric razors in your house," he said. "In case your sister tries to cut herself. You know that, don't you?"

"Why would she cut herself?" I asked, looking at his head.

"It's pretty common," Jimmy said. "Kids in the hospital pick it up."

I was staring at him. He had gone upstairs and found my parents' bedroom and then their bathroom and he had opened the medicine chest and taken my father's razor and used it to shave a path across his head on my parents' back lawn.

"And you should hide the aspirin and all the other drugs. And any booze your parents might have. I bet they've got some booze up there in that cabinet. It's up there, right? Don't worry, I won't drink it." He pointed at the liquor cabinet over the sink, and a collection of short black hairs drifted from the razor in his hand onto the tile floor. I imagined my mother sweeping them up.

"Dora doesn't drink, Jimmy," I said. "She would tell me if she did. And the only drugs she's taking are antidepressants."

"Do you know which ones?"

"No."

"I'd be curious," Jimmy said. "But that's just me. Are the noodles ready? Where do you keep your spices?"

I looked at the pot almost boiling over on the stove. "I'm trying to remember why I called you tonight."

He found two plates in the cabinet and two forks in the drawer. "Maybe you couldn't think of anyone else to call. Did you have other choices?" He pointed a fork in my direction. "You don't talk very much," he said. "I talk more than you do. But maybe there's something you've been wanting to say. Go ahead, I'm listening."

I drained the noodles. The steam rose up from the sink, a cloud of it enclosing both me and Jimmy. "I wonder if being depressed is like being underwater," I said. "Like Dora's trapped underwater and she has to breathe all her air through a straw." Feeling vaguely embarrassed, I dumped the noodles back into the pot.

"I think that's asthma you're talking about," Jimmy said.

"Forget it." I asked if he was going to wash his hands before we ate.

"Sure. Did you want me to say a blessing, too? O Creator

of the Universe, please bless this yellow cheese and these golden noodles—"

"Could you possibly be quiet for a change?" I asked.

"Yeah, I could try," Jimmy said. And for about forty seconds, he did.

22

"Why are these glasses in the sink?" my mother asked when she and my father came home. "Did you have company while we were gone?"

"No." I had washed the plates and the silverware and the pot and the grater but I had forgotten the two drinking glasses.

"You used two glasses just for yourself?" My mother stood over them like a detective searching for evidence.

"Yes," I said. "I drank something twice. I was very thirsty."

My mother took off her shoes and sat down and rubbed her feet. She had been increasingly crabby the past few days. Standing above her, I could see the gray stripe down the part in her hair; she had forgotten to dye it.

"How's Dora?" I asked.

"A little impatient," my mother said. "And a little tired. They're trying a new kind of medication but it makes her drowsy. She liked the book you picked out. I read her a story." My mother looked at the refrigerator door. It was covered with pictures of Dora and me: an almost-two-year-old Dora holding a newborn me on her lap. A Halloween picture in which Dora was a witch and I was a fairy. Both of our school photos from kindergarten on. In the pictures taken of the two of us (at the lake, at my grandparents' house, on the swings at the playground), we looked like two stairsteps: Dora always twenty-one months older and half a head taller.

"I need to call Sheila," my mother said. Sheila was Dora's piano teacher. "I don't know what I'll tell her." She straightened a photo. "You and Dora were always so different. As soon as she was born I could see exactly who she was. She was a fierce little red-faced thing. But you were quieter. You were an observer. As soon as you were old enough to walk, even though you were younger, it seemed *you* were keeping an eye on *her*."

"Mom, why haven't we told anyone?" I asked. "Why don't you just tell Sheila what happened?"

My mother touched the gray stripe in her hair.

I pointed out that no one had sent Dora a get-well card. Even our grandparents didn't know she'd been hospitalized. And I pointed out that when Mr. Franzen, down the block, had open-heart surgery, everyone had brought casseroles to his house and walked his dog until he got better.

"We don't have a dog," my mother said. "So we don't need anyone to walk it."

Leaving out the fact that he'd been in the house half an hour earlier, I told my mother about Jimmy and about his brother; I told her what Jimmy had said about Lorning and about Dr. Siebald.

My mother picked a fleck of cheese off the table. "That sounds like thirdhand information, Lena. And I don't think it's a good idea for you to be consulting the neighbors about your sister."

"But Jimmy's mother is a psychiatrist."

"I remember Jimmy's mother being a little unusual," my mother said. She stood up and put her shoes back on. "I don't want to talk about this anymore. I'm going upstairs. Here: I forgot to give you this." She reached into her pocket and handed me a folded piece of paper. On the front it said, *Miss you too.* I opened it up and turned it over. At the bottom of the page, in Dora's pinched square writing, was a sentence in code: *Aqw bgbl'r amkc. You didn't come.*

23

I wanted to visit, but I couldn't see her on Sunday, either. I had agreed about a month earlier to babysit for our neighbors, the Fentons, that day, and when I tried to back out of it my mother told me it was too late to cancel.

So I wrote Dora another note. I had started writing her notes every day. I wrote them in code and put them in the mailbox or gave them to my mother, who dropped off food and clean clothes at Lorning, even on days when we weren't allowed to visit.

Most of the messages I sent were short and cheery: *Dora—I miss you. Everything is going to be okay. Lila and Kate both want to say hi.*

Once I wrote that exercise and fish oil (I had learned in an article my father had left on the kitchen table) were good for depression. Dora sent back a note with a picture of herself as a long-haired fish lifting a pair of barbells.

K fyrc kv fcpc, she scribbled underneath. *I hate it here.*

24

"Tell me what you're thinking and what you're feeling," the Grandma Therapist said.

Apparently someone had decided—since we were still living through a "period of stress"—that I would have a regular appointment every Tuesday at four-fifteen.

I pushed my spine against the back of my chair. I wished our chairs didn't face each other. Talking to a therapist, I thought, was like taking your clothes off and then taking your skin off, and then having the other person say, "Would you mind opening up your rib cage so that we can start?"

"I don't see what good this is supposed to do," I said. "Our sitting here talking."

The Grandma Therapist nodded. "The idea at first," she said, "is that you start to trust me."

I didn't understand why trust was relevant: it wasn't as if I were telling her secrets. "Dora's been in the hospital," I said.

"I heard. Your mother spoke to me on the phone about that."

"Do you think Lorning is a terrible hospital?" I asked.

"No. But I'm not an expert." The Grandma Therapist looked at me as if it were my turn to talk. It almost always seemed to be my turn. The Grandma Therapist wore white plastic glasses that matched the white of her hair. She wore one silver earring.

A couple of minutes ticked by.

"Where is it coming from?" I asked. I meant Dora's

depression. I understood unhappiness when it came *attached* to something: to someone dying or to a friend moving away or to being disappointed. But Dora's unhappiness—or whatever it was—seemed to exist independently, on its own. I pictured stunted, faceless creatures manufacturing it in a cave somewhere, like a toxic gas.

"I'm not sure what you're asking. Where is what coming from?"

I turned sideways in my chair and kicked at the leg of the little table where she kept the plant and the clock and the tissues and the jar of stones. "Never mind."

"Are you angry about something?"

"No."

"It seems as if you're angry. Or maybe upset. You're not looking at me."

"I'm not upset." Through a slit in the blinds, I could see a slice of gray sky full of clouds. I tried not to picture the Grandma Therapist as a giant ear. "How long does it usually take?" I asked.

"Do you mean, how long does it take for a person to recover from depression?"

I nodded.

"That varies a lot from person to person. Every instance of mental illness is unique."

I took a couple of stones from the jar. "It's not 'mental illness.' "

The Grandma Therapist tilted her head.

"That's not what it's called," I said. "That makes it sound like Dora's crazy."

"I'm not saying your sister is crazy," the Grandma Therapist said. "I wouldn't use that word for anyone."

I kicked the leg of the table again.

She stood up and lifted the table carefully, setting it down out of reach. Then she sat in her chair again, facing me. "You still haven't told me what you're feeling."

"That's because I don't like the word *feeling*," I said.

"Why not?"

I told her about my family reputation for being stoic. "I'm not a crier," I said. "I never cry."

"Maybe that's something we should talk about."

I tried to push myself even farther back in my chair.

"It isn't easy to live with uncertainty." The Grandma Therapist folded her hands. "Maybe you wish you could wave a magic wand and put everything back the way it was."

"I don't want a magic wand." Was she making fun of me? "I just want Dora to get better."

"Of course you do." She slowly leaned toward me, and I felt my heart begin to pound. "But aren't we here primarily to talk about you? About what *you're* going through and how *you're* feeling?"

"No." I looked down at her shoes. They were made of boiled wool or felt and looked like slippers.

"Why not?"

"Because. There's no me without Dora," I explained.

25

That Thursday (Dora had been at Lorning for almost two weeks), I put on my jacket and got into the car before my parents could leave for the hospital. On my lap I had a bag of black licorice strings. Dora loved licorice. On the seat beside me I had her favorite pink-and-white-striped pillow.

My mother opened the front door of the car and poked her head through the opening. She turned and looked at me like a hunter peering down a rabbit hole. "Elena," she said.

"What?" I knew that look well.

"Dora's had a hard couple of days," my mother said.

My father appeared at the driver's-side door and jingled his keys. "Is Elena coming?"

My mother sighed and got into the car, slamming the door and turning around in her seat to show me her *I am warning you* expression. "Try not to say anything to upset her."

"I'm not going to upset her. And I'd appreciate it if you didn't treat me like a six-year-old."

We didn't talk on the way there. We parked and walked through the parking lot and went up in the elevator and approached the metal detector. The security officer—a woman this time—looked at the licorice and squeezed Dora's pillow. "Just checking." She winked.

A nurse answered the buzzer and let us onto the ward, then put her hands on her hips and said, "Dora? Let's see."

She had us wait in a tiny conference room, big enough for one small round table and four plastic chairs. The metal feet on my chair were uneven; they made me rock back and forth. I opened the licorice strings and started to tie them into knots. I thought about spelling Dora's name with them. I thought about the way Dora would roll her eyes when I told her our parents hadn't wanted to let me come.

"Here she is," my father said, and when I looked up I saw the person he had probably mistaken for my sister. She was about the right height but her hair was oily and unwashed and her lips were swollen, chapped, and bloody. She was wearing a pair of shapeless green pants and a hospital gown.

"It's good to see you, sweetheart," my mother said.

The Dora-like person sat down.

My father threw me a look: *Easy does it*.

"Did you have a rough day?" My mother leaned forward in her chair. "You look a little tired. Have you been sleeping?" She tucked Dora's hair behind her ears, wiped something from her face (was Dora crying?), found a tube of lip balm in her pocket, and applied it carefully to Dora's lips. My father and I had both turned to stone.

"It's all right, Daisy Dora," my mother said. "You're just worn out. It'll be all right." Slowly and awkwardly, because Dora was taller and much longer-limbed than she was, my mother pulled Dora onto her lap. Dora sagged against her. "There we go," my mother said. She had turned into the mother I remembered from when I was little, the mother who would come into my room at night when I was sick and scribble pictures on my back with her fingernails. "Sweet Dora," she said. "Lena came to see you."

My father excused himself to get a cup of water.

I passed Dora the licorice ("Hey, Dora") but she didn't seem to notice.

"Should I read to you again?" my mother asked. "Should I read you a story?"

Dora pushed her face into my mother's shoulder. She had bitten her fingernails down so far there was almost nothing left of them.

Clumsily, because she still held Dora on her lap, my mother opened the book she had brought with her: *Classic Fairy Tales for Children,* the book I'd picked out the week before.

My father came back into the room and all of us listened while my mother read from "Snow White." Soon the seven dwarves were weeping around the coffin. Right before the prince came I wrote Dora a note. *Love you,* it said in code. *As big as the sky.*

Dora picked up the crayon—she wasn't allowed to use pencils—and circled one word. *Uma: sky.*

26

"They must have just given her her medications," my father said on our way back to the elevator. "Otherwise she wouldn't have looked so exhausted."

My parents have been lying to me, I thought.

My mother walked in front of us, by herself, the book of fairy tales under her arm.

"They haven't found the right dosage or combination," my father said. "I guess it can take a while sometimes."

They had kept me from seeing her. They hadn't told me what was happening to her. And Jimmy was right about Lorning. I stopped at the trash can and gazed down into its plastic liner. I took a few deep breaths.

The security officer was listening to a baseball game on the radio. On the table beside her were a couple of cigarette lighters, a pin, a pocketknife, and some other things that were too dangerous for people like my sister.

"There are always going to be ups and downs," my father said. "Two steps forward, one step back."

Dora had asked me to save her.

"Stan, let's go. Come on, Elena." My mother got our coats and her purse from the locker and the three of us walked to the elevator, which immediately dinged and let us in.

When we got to the car I opened both the back windows, and even though it was cold no one asked me to close them.

We pulled out of the parking lot and stopped at a light and

I watched the traffic come and go. How could everyone keep driving as if nothing had happened? I wanted to get out of the car and slam the door and stand in the middle of the intersection and stop every single passing vehicle and grab every driver by the collar so I could say, *Look. Look what's happened to my family. Look.*

I went to bed early that night and woke up a few hours later to the sound of my parents engaged in their new hobby: arguing in the kitchen. The kitchen was directly under my bedroom; their voices floated toward me through the vents.

"All I'm saying is that we should ask for another opinion," my father said. "There have to be other options out there."

"Out where?" my mother asked. "We can't be changing our minds every day. We're supposed to be consistent and stay the course."

"*Stay the course?*" My father was shouting. "My god, Gail, she can barely hold her head up. She's drugged to the gills. Have you really looked at her?"

"Do you think I'm blind?" my mother shouted back. "Of course I've looked at her. What else do I spend my time doing?"

My father said something I couldn't hear.

"Better drugged than trying to kill herself," my mother said.

28

Jimmy wasn't at school the next day, so I decided to call him that afternoon when I got off the bus.

"No, I'm sorry. He's out for a bit. Is this Elena? How nice that you've called—really, that's sweet. This is Jimmy's mother, Marilyn. I'm so glad you two are becoming friends."

"Um, yeah. He was absent today so I was just calling to—"

"All these years and you've lived so near each other, just down the street, and now—Well, I'm delighted to see it. Truly. And I want you to know that my son is a very good boy."

"Great," I said. "So maybe you could tell him—"

"He's a person with character. Real moral fiber. I've often told him that he has an old soul. And a lot of horse sense. And that isn't common in a person his age, as I'm sure you know."

"Right," I said. "Would you ask him to call me?"

Adoradora, I wrote. *I'm sorry you weren't feeling well yesterday.* I bit the tip of my pen and switched to code. *If there's anything you need me to do—*

"Someone's at the door for you, Lena," my mother called. "It's a young man."

A young man? I folded up the letter I'd been writing and went down the stairs and saw the familiar jagged black haircut, the torn jeans and T-shirt, the gray-blue eyes. "Hey, Jimmy."

My mother stood in the hall, a department store dummy.

"Mom," I said. "You remember Jimmy Zenk."

"Nice to see you again," my mother said, all cool politeness. "Lena, it's getting late for visitors."

"It's Friday, Mom," I said. "Besides, Jimmy and I are working on a history project together." This was a lie, and my mother probably suspected that it was a lie, but how would she prove it?

Jimmy followed me down the hall and into the kitchen, where he immediately opened the refrigerator. "Are these eggs organic?" he asked. "I could make us an omelet."

"It's nine o'clock, Jimmy. Didn't you have dinner?"

"Yeah, I ate." He closed the refrigerator and pulled out a chair and sat down at the table. "My mom said you called me."

I felt my face flush. "You weren't in school today," I said. "So I was just wondering."

"Wondering what?"

"Why you were absent. Were you sick?"

"No. I had some stuff I needed to do." He was watching me closely.

I sat down across from him. "You're probably absent a lot. I go to school every day," I said.

"Yup." He picked up my index finger and tapped it against the table. "You're pretty faithful."

My mother breezed into the kitchen and noisily poured herself a glass of water. I unfolded the note I'd been writing to Dora and picked up a pencil. "Okay, about Paul Revere," I said. "Was it 'One if by land and two if by sea' or was it the other way around?" My mother left.

"I get the feeling your mother doesn't like me very much," Jimmy said.

"She doesn't," I agreed. I smoothed out the piece of paper. "We went to see Dora last night."

"Yeah?" Jimmy stood up and paced around the kitchen, picking up a jar full of sunflower seeds. "These are good for you, right?"

I said they probably were. "She didn't look good," I said. "My mom read her a story. A fairy tale for little kids."

Jimmy unscrewed the lid of the jar and tossed back a handful of sunflower seeds. "Are you okay?"

"I wasn't talking about me."

"I noticed." Jimmy had a scar at the corner of his mouth that made his upper lip slightly uneven. He tossed back another handful of seeds.

"Most people don't know what it's like," I said.

"Then tell me. What is it like?" Jimmy leaned against the cabinet, crossing his legs.

"I think it's like a trapdoor," I said. "Dora's depression—

it's like a trapdoor under her feet. Sometimes the trapdoor is closed and she walks right by it, but all of a sudden one day it opens and she plunges through. And there she is, walking around underneath us, under the life she's supposed to be living, but she can't find a ladder and she can't get back." I started doodling on the piece of paper. "I guess that's my metaphor for the day."

"It was a simile," Jimmy said. "If you use the word *like* it's a simile."

I stared at him. "How do you know things like that?" I asked.

"I keep my ears open," Jimmy said. "I stay alert." He screwed the lid back onto the jar and set it down by the stove. "Can I have some water?"

"Sure. Glasses are behind you." I started to wish that I hadn't called him. "Did everything turn out all right with your brother?" I asked. "I don't remember his name."

"Mark?" Jimmy filled up a glass. "Mark lives in Cleveland."

"Oh. Is that good?"

"For him it is. He wants to be an EMT—you know, one of the guys in the ambulance who shows up when you dial 9-1-1."

"That's great. Well, thanks for coming over, Jimmy," I said.

"Do you want me to leave now? Am I dismissed?"

I shrugged.

He noticed the paper I'd been doodling on. He turned it toward him. "What is this?" he asked.

"It's just a note," I said. "Sometimes I write them to Dora in code."

"You write code," Jimmy said.

I looked at his mangled hair and the uneven place on his lip and I ended up explaining how it worked—two letters forward in the first word, two letters back.

"Write me a sentence," Jimmy said.

I wrote him a sentence. *Kv dccjq tgcnna jmlcjw.* He took the pencil out of my hand. I watched his lips move while he figured it out.

Finally he nodded. "You don't need to feel lonely right now," he said.

I felt a tightening at the back of my throat, but I fought it down.

My mother's voice found its way into the kitchen. "Are you two working on your history project?"

30

That night I had a dream that a genie who looked like Mr. Clearwater came out from behind the bathroom mirror in a cloud of blue smoke and offered me three wishes, and after I wished for world peace and an end to global warming and the melting of the ice caps, he clapped his hands and said, "That's three" (counting global warming and the ice caps separately instead of together), and then he yelled at me and told me I'd forgotten Dora. "What on earth were you thinking?" he asked, twirling his mustache and fading back into the mirror.

I got out of bed. Dora used to complain that our lives were too ordinary. She used to say we needed more adventure, more unexpectedness, maybe more of a thrill. But I wanted our lives to be ordinary, to be built out of ordinary things: Dora feeding bologna to the fish at Nevis Pond; Dora making me a pancake with a swear word baked into the batter; Dora and I painting our toenails together on the bathroom floor.

It was 4 a.m. I went downstairs and found my father in his pajamas in the kitchen, reading the paper. The cat, Mr. Peebles, was crunching on something in his dish.

"Yesterday's news," my father said, turning a page. He didn't seem surprised to see me. "It's still too early for today's."

I sat down across from him at the table. The hair on one

side of his head was sticking out. "Do you want to work on the crossword?" he asked.

"No. I'm not good at puzzles." I had never sat in the kitchen in the middle of the night before. "I don't think we should leave her there," I said.

I thought my father would tell me that I shouldn't worry, that everything would work out. But he only nodded and folded the paper.

Mr. Peebles crept under the table, rubbing in a figure eight pattern against my legs.

"How about some breakfast?" my father asked.

31

On Saturday I called the Grandma Therapist's answering machine, because I thought the sound of her voice might help me think. "If you are in crisis," the message said, "please call the emergency hotline at the following number." I pressed the receiver to my ear and thought about the Grandma Therapist's fuzzy shoes and the way she sometimes tilted her head when we talked. What exactly did she mean by *crisis*? And what did she think I ought to do about Dora?

"I wish you well," the message ended. "We'll be in touch."

At the sound of the beep I hung up and immediately redialed. "Hello. You have reached the office of—"

"Who are you calling?" my mother asked. She had come up behind me in the kitchen.

"No one." I hung up.

"You were standing there for such a long time."

"It wasn't that long," I said.

My mother straightened out a pile of papers on the kitchen counter. "I meant to ask you how your therapy appointments are going."

"They're fine." Did she somehow know who I'd been calling?

"Because we can find someone else for you to talk to if you'd rather." She opened an envelope. "Are the appointments . . . helpful?"

I wasn't sure—I didn't know what they were supposed to

accomplish. When I was in the Grandma Therapist's office, I generally wanted to be anywhere else. When I wasn't in her office, I often found myself thinking about her coiled rug and her jar of stones.

"There are a lot of therapists out there to choose from," my mother said. "You want someone you can talk to."

I told her I might as well stick with the person I had.

32

"You're much more alert this time, Rabbit," my father said. More black licorice tied into knots, and more fairy tales. "You had us worried last Thursday." We were in the conference room again, with the door propped open. Now and then one of the other kids would pause to stare at us until the nurses came to shoo them away.

"They changed my dosage," Dora said. "I think they screwed it up for a while." Her hair was still oily and uncombed, and her collarbones jutted out under her skin above the neck of her hospital gown; still, she looked brighter, more like herself. "They're going to discharge me this week," she added.

"They said they'd discharge you?" my father asked.

"Yeah. They said something about it." Dora bit into a knotted hunk of licorice.

"That's great," my father said. "Great news." I could tell he was trying not to look surprised.

"Completely wonderful." My mother smiled.

Dora picked at a scab on her lip. Because we didn't seem to have enough to talk about, my mother started reading from *Classic Fairy Tales for Children*. I wrote Dora a note in code with an orange crayon while my mother read from "Cinderella": *Can't wait till you're back. Am bored by myself. Mom has at least 3 personalities.*

Dora glanced over my shoulder, chewing on licorice. She

read and wrote code much faster than I could. *What else is new?* she quickly scrawled.

The prince was knocking on doors, looking for eligible feet and for the moment when he would live happily ever after.

My father was leafing through a copy of *Hospital Weekly*.

Dora picked up her crayon. *Mom and Dad won't trust me anymore,* she wrote.

They will, I scribbled back. *Are you excited to leave?*

"What are the two of you writing?" my father asked. He looked at our messages. "It's not fair to keep secrets."

"Is anyone listening to this story?" my mother asked.

"Yeah. We can't wait to find out what happens," Dora said. "The suspense is killing me."

"Very funny." My mother put her finger in the book and closed it, but Dora asked her to keep reading. One of the stepsisters cut off her little toe.

My father closed his eyes and leaned back in his chair. Dora waggled the crayon and wrote *nervous.*

Cdqwv ufyr? I asked. *About what?*

Not sure, she wrote.

My mother finished with "Cinderella."

"I love happy endings," Dora said. One of the nurses came to say that our time was up.

Now everything will go back to the way it was, I wrote, as fast as I could. But Dora stood up and left the note on the table, so I wasn't sure whether she ended up reading it or not.

33

She came home in the middle of October, on a Saturday, after twenty-two days on the psychiatric ward at Lorning. The leaves had turned while she was gone. From the living room window, I watched her unfold her skinny long-legged self from the car and look up at the house. She scanned each window, left to right, as if she were trying to read it and memorize it. In her arms she carried a paper bag full of clothes and her favorite pillow. I opened the door and watched her walk toward me. "Hey there," I said.

"Hey yourself. I'm back from the hellhole." She gave me a one-armed hug.

My mother asked her not to swear.

Dora took a long shower while my parents and I all pretended not to wait for her, and then the four of us ate lunch together. It felt awkward and formal (we didn't normally eat lunch as a family), and none of us seemed to know what to say. Dora tucked her long damp hair into the back of her T-shirt, slid her collection of silver bracelets (she had gotten them back) along her wrist, and started to talk about a kid at the hospital whose parents had sexually abused him, so that he ended up in foster care. My mother interrupted her and changed the subject. "I'm going to plant some bulbs this afternoon," she said. She went on and on about where she was going to plant the bulbs and how she was going to make sure that squirrels wouldn't dig them up. My father nodded and listened as if he would be tested on the subject later.

I felt as if I were eating lunch with someone else's family—with a group of well-meaning but unpredictable strangers.

"We could go for a walk this afternoon," my father said. "Or maybe Dora wants to call a friend?"

Dora took a couple of her bracelets off and rearranged them. "No. I'm pooped. I'm going to take a nap." She went up to her room and slept until dinner.

At six o'clock we were sitting around the table again, my father offering a rambling description of his plan to fix the bird feeder. Dora sat next to me and ate almost nothing. Her arms were bony, as narrow as blades.

I decided to fill up the air in front of us with a description of a food fight in the cafeteria at school and a story about a girl in my gym class piercing her belly button with a needle; and then without thinking about it I described one of the quirky, aimless conversations I'd had on the bus that week with Jimmy.

"Jimmy?" Dora pulled back her thick hay-colored hair as if removing a barrier between us. "Do you mean Jimmy Zenk?"

"I was only talking to him," I said.

Dora crushed a lima bean with her fork. "Interesting," she said. "You don't like him, do you? You know he was left back at least once. There's something weird about that family."

"He's in my history class," I said. "Don't make a big deal of it."

"I don't think I'm making a big deal. I just asked you a question."

"You asked me two questions."

"Let's make it three, then," Dora said. "Why are you hanging out with Jimmy Zenk?"

"Does 'hanging out' mean dating?" my mother asked. "You aren't dating him, are you?"

I crumpled my napkin and put it in the center of my plate. "May I be excused?"

"After you clear the dishes, you may be excused," my mother said. Her tone suggested that I barely spoke English.

"I've cleared them about a hundred times in a row now," I said.

"That's because you weren't locked up in a psych ward," Dora said. She licked her fork. "Like lucky me."

34

The next morning there were half a dozen pills lined up on the kitchen counter for Dora, a little multicolored cluster.

"What are all those for?" I asked.

"They're to keep me from turning into a werewolf." Dora picked up a bread knife and clutched it in her fist. *"Someone stop me before I kill again!"* She swallowed the pills with a glass of juice. "God, those are tasty. You really should try some." Half an hour later, at 10 a.m., she was asleep on the couch.

"They're still working some of the kinks out of her medications," my father said. "And I'm sure she's tired. It's hard to sleep in a hospital."

I wondered whether Lorning had changed Dora. "Do you think we should hide her pills?" I asked.

"Your mother's taking care of that," he said.

I looked up at the cabinet over the sink, where my parents kept some wine and a bottle of gin.

"It's great having her back," my father said. "Isn't it?"

I agreed that it was.

He put his arm around my shoulders. "You know we're all counting on you," he said. "You're the steady Eddie of this group."

I nodded.

"There might be a period of adjustment," my father said. "But the worst is behind us." He gave me a squeeze. "We got through it. Right?"

35

Jimmy called me that afternoon as I was doing my home-work. "How are things going so far?" he asked. "How's the reentry?"

"Okay, I guess." I carried the phone into my bedroom. "She sleeps a lot."

"How much is a lot?" I could picture him running the palm of his hand across his hair.

I told him I wasn't counting the hours. "We just want to put all this behind us."

"Yeah, that makes sense," Jimmy said. "Do your parents have to take time off from work this week to stay home with her?"

"What do you mean?" I flopped down on my bed. "She's going to school. You'll see her tomorrow. She'll be on the bus."

There was a silence. "Going back to school so soon will probably be hard for her," Jimmy said.

"What else is she going to do?" I asked. "She's a kid. Kids go to school."

"Yeah, mostly they do," Jimmy said. Another silence. "My mother might be willing to talk to your parents."

I remembered what my mother had said about Marilyn Zenk. "I don't think my parents want to talk to anyone. Besides, Dora seems fine, mostly. Tired but fine. And my parents seem fine. And I guess I'm fine also."

"Glad to hear it," Jimmy said. "Unanimity. Family har-mony. Very impressive."

"Are you making fun of me?" I asked.

"Yeah. Is that going to bother you?"

I thought about it for a minute. "No," I said. "Probably not."

"That's what I like about you," Jimmy said.

"What?"

"Hang on a second." I heard him talking to someone— probably his mother. "Okay, sorry," he said, coming back to the phone.

I wanted to ask him what he liked about me, but I didn't know how to raise the subject. So I told him I'd see him on the bus, and I hung up the phone.

The next morning at breakfast, Dora contemplated the multicolored pills on the kitchen counter. She took the first pill while my mother watched. She took the second pill and the third. "Ho-hum," she said, swallowing the rest of the pills all at once with a glass of juice.

Then she handed my mother the empty glass and turned to me and showed me the pills in a little wet cluster under her tongue.

We walked to the bus stop together over a carpet of leaves. The air was cold and smelled somehow of metal. "Do I look bad?" Dora asked.

"No."

"Maybe that's because you're looking at my feet."

I stopped walking and faced her. Dora was five inches taller than I was so I had to look *up,* which might have made the bags under her eyes seem bigger. "You're pale," I said. "But not very."

"Pale is okay," Dora said. "Pale is acceptable." We kept walking. "The only pills I didn't take are the ones that make me tired," she said. "In case that's why you're sulking."

"I'm not sulking." The morning was gray; clouds were collecting in layers above us. "I don't think you should do that, though," I said. "Mom thinks you swallowed them." Dora had spit the pills into the bushes when we left the house.

"I need to stay awake at school, for god's sake," Dora said. "I'll be behind in all my classes."

"You're going to catch up fast," I told her. Our mother had written her a note that said, *Please excuse Dora Lindt for her lengthy absence. She was ill.*

Dora took off her backpack and unzipped it. "Do you know what one of the nurses at the hospital told me? She said I was selfish and self-indulgent. She said I was putting my entire family through a very hard time."

"The nurse doesn't know you, Dora," I said.

"Nobody knows me." Dora rooted through her backpack.

I wanted to tell her that *I* knew her. Didn't I? "You should probably tell Mom you didn't swallow those pills," I said.

She didn't answer.

"What are you looking for?" I asked. "We're going to miss the bus."

"I don't give a shit about the bus." Dora folded a stick of gum into her mouth. Her hands were shaking. "If you want to tell Mom I didn't take the pills you can go ahead. I'm not going to stop you." She zipped up her backpack. "If you want to rat on me and watch Mom get all bent out of shape, that's your decision. I'm just trying to stay awake at school like everyone else." She was looking at me, tight-lipped, trembling, waiting.

We were both waiting. Leaves were falling from the tree above us.

"It's okay," I said. "I'm not going to tell."

"Thanks, Elvin," Dora said. "Sorry if I've been a jerk lately."

"You aren't a jerk."

We started walking again. "Being in a piss-poor mood is one of the side effects of some of these drugs," Dora said. "Freaking mood swings and irritability. Did I mention that?"

"No, but I guess I'm finding out about it," I said.

We cut across the Baylors' yard and saw Mr. Baylor in his bathrobe at the kitchen window. He lifted his newspaper and pretended not to see us.

"Wacky old buzzard," Dora said.

The bus was out on the main road with its blinker on. Dora grabbed my sleeve at the elbow and ran. "Pick it up. Move your legs!" she yelled, holding on to me and laughing. "Come on, Layton, can't you *run?*"

86

A good day. Two good days. Dora went to school and came home and didn't seem to care about the kids who gawked and whispered about her in the hall. At dinner, she entertained us with an imitation of her science teacher, Mr. Pflaum.

And then a bad day. Dora refused to get out of bed. My mother called in sick to work, brought Dora's pills upstairs in a cup, and told me to eat something before I went to school.

As a precaution, my mother said (not that anything was wrong, and not that Dora wasn't doing well, because of course she was), my parents had decided to sign all four of us up for family therapy.

"You've got to be kidding," Dora said.

"Of course I'm not kidding." My mother smiled a tight little smile. "It'll give us a chance to talk to each other. And to meet other families. Families who might be going through . . ."

"Going through what?" Dora asked. She was back to picking at her fingers.

"Well, through something similar. To what we're going through."

When Dora asked what "we" were going through, my mother said she would rather get into that conversation at a later time.

The group met on the fourth Friday of every month at Lorning. ("My favorite place. They have such a nice mental ward," Dora said.) On our way to our first session, she draped one of her legs across my lap and fell asleep in the car.

The group—about eighteen of us—met in a conference room with a low, pockmarked ceiling. We sat in a circle of plastic chairs. The girl on my right had a lot of metal in her face and what looked like a homemade tattoo on the side of her neck. I couldn't tell what it was. Maybe a bat or a butterfly.

Dora passed me a note by scribbling something on a slip

of paper, then crumpling it up and dropping it at my feet. I picked it up. *K jmtc jgt yaacqqmpgcq,* it said. *I love her accessories.* Dora had drawn an arrow pointing toward the tattooed girl.

The woman who was running the group—I noticed that she blinked every few seconds as if wearing ill-fitting contact lenses—asked us to reflect about our family's methods of communication.

After several minutes of discussion, the family across from us tried to agree that they wouldn't yell at each other as often. "Not so much as we're used to," the mother said.

The blinking woman said she thought everyone in the room could probably benefit from the family's comments. Calm and consistent ways of speaking were especially important for people with depression and mood swings, she said.

I took a pen out of my pocket and wrote back to Dora. *Aqw lctcp vqnf kc: yjcv gq kv jgic vq ʒc fgrtguugf? You never told me: what is it like to be depressed?* I crumpled the note and tossed it under her chair. She quickly stepped on it without looking. A minute later, she bent as if to scratch her leg, then picked the note up.

One of the fathers on the opposite side of the circle complained that kids didn't listen to their parents anymore. He said that personally he was sick of it; he was sick of his son coming in late and going who knew where with his sloppy friends, all of them sloppy and rude like his son—they had no self-respect.

The boy who must have been his son didn't even react. He wore the hood of his sweatshirt pulled forward so that it hid almost all of his face, and he didn't seem to notice that his father had spoken.

Another crumpled piece of paper landed by my feet. I dragged it under my chair with my sneaker while the parents in the family that had agreed not to yell so much began to shout at each other.

I reached down and opened my sister's note. In the middle of the paper Dora had written the word *sad* (*ucf*) and crossed it out. Lower down and to the side she'd written *small* and crossed it out. Then, at the bottom of the page, in pinched-looking letters in the corner, she'd written *nospace nolight noair*.

The blinking woman called a five-minute break. I put the note in my pocket and went out to the hall and found the girl with the homemade tattoo taking out some serious anger against a vending machine. "Do you have any money on you?" she asked.

I had a dollar but told her I didn't.

Dora sauntered out into the hallway. "Look," she said. "That's Siebald. That guy over there with the little goatee." She waved. "I guess he's busy. He's off to ruin somebody's life now. Bye, Dr. Siebald! See you in therapy!"

The tattooed girl laughed.

"Why don't you get a different doctor if you hate him so much?" I asked Dora.

The tattooed girl answered. "Because all psychiatrists are crazy. That's why they're psychiatrists." She looked at Dora. "Have you got anything on you?"

I thought she was still asking for vending machine money, but Dora understood her. "All my meds are at home," she said. "Sorry."

"Next time," the girl said. She touched a metal stud in her lip. "How many times were you in?" she asked.

"Once," Dora said. "How about you?"

The girl held up three fingers, then walked away.

"I'd rather drown myself in a sink than go back to Lorning," Dora said.

"You wouldn't have given her any pills," I said. "Would you?"

"What do you think?" Dora asked.

"I think it would be stupid."

She grabbed my jeans by the belt loops. "And are you calling me stupid?"

"No."

"Good." She shook me gently, jerking the belt loops back and forth. "Everything I tell you is confidential, Lay-Lay," she said. "Every single syllable."

I nodded.

"You're the only person I can trust. There's no one else. I need to trust you."

I told her not to worry. She could.

The good days outnumbered the bad ones, which seemed important. In my mind I tried to stack the better days against the days when I came home and found Dora in bed, or the day when I found her in the kitchen standing in front of the sink with the water running.

"What are you doing, Dora?" I asked.

"I don't know," she said.

I reached around her and turned off the water.

When the Grandma Therapist asked me how my sister was doing, I felt it was important to be loyal to Dora, so I said fine.

"Hey." Dora's friend Lila stopped me in the hall by a long row of lockers. It was a Wednesday in late October. Dora had been home for eleven days. "I just thought I should mention something. You know, maybe it's none of my business. But Dora isn't in class as often anymore."

"She's been taking some sick days," I said. "And sometimes she has a doctor's appointment. It's not a big deal."

"Yeah, I figured." Lila removed a hair from her sweater. "But I'm talking about the days when she's here at school. Like today. She's in the building somewhere but she isn't in class."

"What do you mean, she isn't in class?" I felt as if my entire body had been dipped in a vat of cold water.

"We're in the same math and the same science," Lila said, "and she used to cut class once in a while, but now it happens a lot. She wasn't there last period. She missed yesterday, too."

Someone bumped into me with an armload of books. I looked at Lila's perfect smooth straight black hair and the perfect clothes she had picked out that morning, the beaded necklace and bracelet that matched. *This could have happened to you,* I thought. *This could have happened to you instead of my sister.*

"I have to go," Lila said. "But I wanted to tell you. You know, in case."

In case of what? I had always liked Lila but now I wanted to uncap the marker I kept in my pocket and write something obscene on the front of her sweater. "Do you know where she goes?" I asked. "When she's not in class?"

Lila was already walking away. "I think she hangs out in the bathrooms sometimes," she said.

42

"Dora? Are you in here?"

There were two girls' bathrooms on the first floor, one on the second, and one on the third. It took me nine minutes, running up the stairs, to look in each one.

"Dora?"

No answer. I didn't even know which classes she had decided to cut.

43

"Don't flip out on me," Dora said. "I'm not ditching that often. I just need to think sometimes."

"Oh," I said. "About what?" We were walking home from the bus stop. It was almost Halloween, and a couple of little kids in costumes were running around on the neighbors' front lawn.

"I can't sit there hour after hour with people talking at me." She moved her hands in the air like little puppets. "It all seems so pointless."

"Why is it pointless?" School could be boring sometimes, I thought, but as long as you went to class and read and learned things, it was hard to argue that it didn't have a point.

Mr. Peebles was waiting on the front porch for us, cleaning his whiskers and looking annoyed.

"I think I'm failing French," Dora said.

I dug my house key out of my pocket. "You could get a tutor."

"Yeah. Except that I'm also failing chemistry. I hate Mrs. King. She's a walking fossil." Dora picked Mr. Peebles up and scratched his furry stomach. "You probably have all As, don't you?"

"No." I had a B in biology. I opened the door; the house was quiet. "How are you ditching and not getting caught?" I asked when Dora put Mr. Peebles down. "Doesn't the office call home when you're missing?"

"They only call if you don't have a written excuse."

"And?"

Dora paused, then opened her backpack and showed me a note on my mother's new monogrammed stationery: *Please excuse Dora Lindt at 11:35 today; she has a doctor's appointment.*

I looked at the signature; it was almost perfect. "You could get in a lot of trouble for this."

"Maybe. But the only way that would happen"—Dora tore up the note—"would be if someone found out and told the school."

44

"I think being at school is hard for her," I said to my mother while we were folding laundry. It was Saturday and I had offered to help. Matching socks was generally acknowledged to be my specialty.

"You worry about your schoolwork, and Dora can worry about hers," my mother said. "You look like you're turning into a statue."

I had started playing a mental game that involved touching each sock only once: after a sock had been touched, I had to find its mate without touching any other article of clothing first. I was holding a white gym sock in my hand; in front of me on my parents' bed were about a hundred other white socks.

"I'm not talking about schoolwork, though," I said. "I'm talking about being in the building. For seven hours in a row—it's pretty stressful."

"She can hardly stay *outside* the building," my mother said.

"Yeah. That would be weird." I picked up another white sock—luckily it matched—and folded the two elastic tops together. "The thing is," I said, but just then my father came into the bedroom. He kissed me on the forehead and handed my mother two bottles of pills. "Where's Dora?" he asked.

My mother tilted her head in the direction of Dora's bedroom door, which was closed. We could hear loud music, mainly the throbbing bass of the speakers.

I picked up a sock. "What are the pills for?" I asked.

"Dora's prescriptions," my father said. "They're going to try something new."

"What kind of pills are they?"

My father opened his mouth to answer, but before he could say anything, my mother held up her hand: "I don't think Elena needs to know that."

My father closed his mouth and pretended to zip it.

"Why are they trying something new?" I asked. "How would they know if something was wrong with the old pills?" I held a striped sock in one hand and a plain one in the other.

My mother tucked the pills in her pocket and shook out a pillowcase with a snap. "What are you getting at?"

"Nothing. So are the new pills antidepressants?"

"I'll be downstairs if anyone needs me," my father said. He left the room.

I decided to segregate ankle- from kneesocks. "Maybe you should get Dora a different psychiatrist," I said.

"I don't think so." My mother shook out another pillow-case.

"Jimmy's mother hated Dr. Siebald."

"That's enough, Lena."

"Jimmy says the doctors at Lorning just lock the kids up and give them drugs, and if we don't even know whether the pills Dora's been taking do her any good—"

"I said *that's enough!*" My mother was clutching the rim of the laundry basket. "Whatever you're trying to say, I don't want to hear it. It doesn't help to have you latching on to half-baked theories that you've picked up at school from people who wouldn't know a hospital from a hole in the ground. I don't have time for that, Elena."

Maybe you should make the time, I thought. I left the socks where they were and went back to my room.

About ten minutes later I heard my mother carry the laundry basket downstairs. I listened for footsteps and the clink of dishes in the kitchen. Then I went into my parents' room and opened their closet and unzipped the outer compartment of my mother's blue suitcase. She always hid our birthday presents inside it. I found the two bottles. *Lindt, Dora,* each of them said. I copied down the information from the labels and zipped the prescriptions back into the suitcase.

The music pounded, louder and louder, in Dora's room.

45

The new pills (she started taking them the next morning) didn't make Dora drowsy. They made her angry. She called my father a jackass.

"You people don't give a crap about me," she said.

I'd already promised she could trust me. Who did she mean by *you people?*

46

"Were you checking the bathrooms again?" Jimmy asked.

I had just flopped down at the desk next to his. We were in Mr. Clearwater's room, supposedly reading the morning paper. Every Monday we spent the first fifteen minutes of the period trying to find relevant or "stimulating" articles about current events. Most of the kids read the comics or did the puzzle.

"If you keep this up, your teachers are going to think you've got dysentery." Jimmy crossed his legs at the knee and leaned back in his chair, the newspaper open on his lap. He actually read it; other than the faded long-sleeved T-shirt and the partly shaved head, he looked like a businessman on his lunch break. "Besides," he said, "didn't you tell me that you hate to miss class?"

"I should probably be checking the locker room," I said. I was still breathing hard. "But Dora doesn't like gym."

Mr. Clearwater decided to get out from behind his desk and circumnavigate like Columbus around the room. He was jiggling a piece of chalk in his hand. "Mr. Zenk? I'm sure you won't mind if I ask you to cease and desist from all conversation."

"Right," said Jimmy.

"Ms. Lindt?" Mr. Clearwater paused beside my desk, still jiggling his chalk. "Are you finding anything illuminating or relevant in this morning's news?"

I pushed my hair behind my ears and stared at the newspaper on my desk. "I'm still looking," I said.

"Good. You don't want to give up." Mr. Clearwater leaned toward me, his pointed mustache approaching my face, and turned the page. Only after he was back in his chair at the front of the room did I notice that he had left a chalky thumbprint in the left-hand corner of an article about depression. *Teenage Epidemic?* the headline asked. And beneath the headline, in smaller letters: *How Safe Are the Drugs?*

I tore the article out (Mr. Clearwater pretended not to notice) and wrote Jimmy a note in the upper margin: *Vcnm ml vjg ʒsq?* Then I watched him slowly puzzle it out. *Talk on the bus?*

47

A bunch of guys hooted and whistled when I sat on the last torn seat by the emergency exit, next to Jimmy. *"Hey, Jimmy Zee! Getting some action?"*

Jimmy ignored them. "What's up?" he asked. He smelled like soap.

I was full of a nagging uneasy feeling. A stand of gray trees flickered by through my window. Dora wasn't on the bus. My mother had picked her up earlier for a doctor's appointment.

"Remember you asked me about the kinds of medicines Dora was taking?"

Jimmy nodded. The bus dragged itself up a hill.

"I wrote the names down," I said. We had reached the first stop. The bus doors opened with a wheeze and closed with a sigh. In the seventh grade I'd seen a movie about the human heart, and ever since, I'd thought that a bus door opening looked like the valve of a heart when the blood was pumped through. "I have them here in my pocket."

We stopped at a light. I found the piece of paper where I had written down the names of the drugs and I showed it to Jimmy. I had even remembered to write down the doses. "So? What do you think?"

Jimmy barely glanced at it. "I think . . . that I'm not a pharmacist," he said. "You haven't asked, but I might as well tell you: I'm planning to be a chef. I'm going to open my own restaurant. You can come if you want—I'll save you a table."

We went over a bump; my leg pressed against his. I put the piece of paper back in my pocket. "I'll eat in your restaurant," I said. "But in the meantime, would you help me find out about these pills?"

48

Chocolate milk with club soda. I was almost beginning to like the taste.

"Jimmy, I thought you were going to help me with this," I said.

"I am helping." He had set me up with a laptop at his kitchen table.

"You aren't helping. You're cooking."

"This is just a snack," Jimmy said. "But it looks pretty good." He had spread an assortment of crackers with a mixture of cream cheese and horseradish and capers (what the heck were capers?) and dusted the top of each with some kind of spice.

I looked back at the computer screen. The Web sites I had found so far were confusing. They talked about "suicidal ideation" and the side effects of antidepressants: weight loss, weight gain, nausea, dry mouth, dizziness, sweating, tremors, sleep disturbances, mood changes, blurred vision, kidney failure, seizures, and yawning. *Yawning?* One of the Web sites warned about the danger of any antidepressant prescribed to anyone under eighteen.

"You're going to love these," Jimmy said, putting a wooden platter of tiny open-faced sandwiches near me on the table and sitting down. "What have you found out so far?"

"I don't know," I said.

He looked at my hands, which were in my lap instead of

on the laptop. "Did you try asking the computer to help you?"

I pushed it toward him. He ate a cracker. Then, with his mouth full, he said, "Maybe you should decide what it is you want to find out. And what you don't want to find out."

"What do you mean?"

"Forget it. Here." He handed me a cracker. "You've got to try one of these. The fresh pepper is crucial."

I ate a small bite—a corner of a cracker.

"Do your parents know she's ditching class?" Jimmy asked, starting to type.

"My parents are impossible to talk to. And Dora told me not to tell them. I don't want them sending her back to Lorning."

"There are worse things than Lorning," Jimmy said. "Besides, if she had a relapse they could send her somewhere else. They could send her to an RTC out of state."

"What's an RTC?"

"A residential treatment center." Jimmy kept typing. "Like a halfway house."

"So it's like a jail?"

"No. It's a treatment center. Like the one near the Superstop, except that that one is for alcoholics. You aren't eating your snack."

I lowered my voice. "We're not going to send Dora away to live with alcoholics." I pictured my sister in a run-down shack in the woods with a bunch of old men.

"Okay, whatever," Jimmy said. "Here's one of her prescriptions. And it's got a black box."

"A black box?" I pulled the laptop toward me. "Do you mean, like the ones on airplanes?"

Jimmy looked at me as if to see whether I was joking.

"Um, no. A black box is a warning. It means that anyone taking these pills should be kept 'under close observation.' There's an increased risk of suicide." He pointed to the screen. " 'Especially during the first few weeks.' "

I stared at the laptop. "Close observation," I repeated. "What do they mean by 'close'?"

Jimmy picked up a cracker with a mound of stuff on it. "Open your mouth."

I took a bite. The stuff on the cracker tasted bizarre—lumpy and salty—like some sort of cross between a vegetable and a squid.

"It means someone needs to watch her," Jimmy said. "Whenever they switch her meds like that, you have to be careful. Someone should keep an eye on her."

I remembered what my mother had said: from an early age, even though I was younger, it had seemed to be up to me to keep an eye on Dora.

"These might be too salty," Jimmy said, pulling a murky green sphere from his cracker. "Do you think I used too many capers?"

"Dora doesn't swallow her pills sometimes," I said. Because I was nervous, I stuffed an entire cracker into my mouth.

Jimmy closed the laptop. "Say that again?"

"I don't know whether she's still doing it," I said, trying to chew and talk at the same time. "But I saw her put them under her tongue and then spit them out."

"Do you know if she's saving them?" he asked.

I was going to ask him why she would save them, but the pepper and horseradish collided at the back of my throat and squeezed off my airway as if someone inside me had turned off a faucet. I managed to take one small sip of air before I started to cough.

"If you're choking, just make the international sign for it," Jimmy said, holding his hands in front of his throat. "Because I know how to do the Heimlich. I took a one-day course." He watched me cough for a while (he seemed to be hoping for an opportunity to show off his Heimlich maneuver skills), then finally shuffled off to the sink for a glass of water.

I drank most of it down and wiped my eyes while Jimmy watched.

"Are you crying?" he asked.

"No, I'm coughing." I drank the rest of the water. "I never cry. My therapist wants to talk to me about it."

"You never cry?"

I shook my head. "I've never liked the way it feels. It always reminds me of throwing up. You get little signals in your mouth. That watery feeling. It's the same with crying. I don't want to go there."

"Huh. I kind of like crying—not that I do it all the time," Jimmy said. "It's like, 'Hey, look at that, there's salt water coming out of my eyes.'" He ate another cracker. "I'll bet you that crying is actually healthy. You know the human body is about sixty percent water? It's almost the same percentage that the earth is ocean."

"I'm not sure where you're going with that," I said.

He put his hands in his pockets. In black ink, one pocket said *right hand here*. The other said *other hand*. "How are you doing right now?" He cocked his head. "Sixty-five percent water? Seventy percent?"

Why on earth did I tell him anything? I stared at the scar on his lip to make him feel bad.

He touched the scar with his tongue. "How long have you been going to a therapist?"

"Not very long. Forget I said anything about it."

"Don't worry. I'm not going to tell anyone. I'm good with secrets. But therapy's probably a good plan for you," he said.

"I should go home now." I stood up. "Have *you* ever been to a therapist?"

"Who, me?" Jimmy laughed. "My mom's in the field."

49

"Do you think you're yawning a lot?" I asked Dora. I had found her sitting on the couch when I got back from Jimmy's. I imagined a black box inside her, like some kind of new and mysterious organ.

"I don't know," Dora said. "I yawn when I'm tired."

The TV was on but we kept the sound low: we needed to slip past my mother's anti-TV radar.

"Are you sweating?" I asked. "I mean, more than usual?"

"What do you mean, am I sweating? Do I look like I'm sweating?"

"No."

A commercial for sleeping pills came on. Dora pulled her feet up onto the couch, her bracelets jingling.

"Do you have tremors?"

"Jesus, Lena, give it a rest." She shook out a blanket and lay down on the couch. "I'm going to take a nap. Scram."

I turned the TV off and went into the kitchen. My mother was putting on her jacket and collecting her purse. "I need to run to the grocery store," she said. "Dinner at six-thirty."

"Okay."

"You'll leave me a note if you go anywhere?"

"I'm not going anywhere." I wondered if we were speaking in code, if my mother was telling me to *keep an eye on Dora*.

I read the comics and the horoscope ("The events you have been looking forward to will not take place as expected") and went back to the study. "Dora?"

Where she had been napping on the couch, I saw only an indentation on a pillow.

I checked the living room. Empty.

I went to the bottom of the stairs. "Dora?" I ran up the steps and saw that the bathroom door was closed. The water was running. "Dora?" I rattled the knob.

I ran back to my bedroom, found a nail file, and stuck it in the lock.

She was in the tub. She looked up at me, amazed, then took the headphones out of her ears. "What the hell's wrong with you?" she asked, pulling the curtain. "Can't you leave me alone?"

50

"You look a bit nervous today," the Grandma Therapist said. "Are you feeling nervous?"

"No." My knee was bobbing up and down.

"Would you tell me if you did feel nervous?"

"Maybe." Sometimes when I talked to the Grandma Therapist I imagined that my entire body was covered with little invisible doors and it was my job to make sure they didn't open.

"I get the impression you aren't used to confiding in people," the Grandma Therapist said. "You like to keep things bottled up. Do you think that strategy is working for you?"

Sometimes, though she was a mild-mannered person, I found the Grandma Therapist terrifying. "I'm not going to fall apart worrying about things that won't happen," I said.

The Grandma Therapist waited.

"You asked if I was nervous," I explained. "And so I'm saying that even if I *was* nervous, I would be okay. Because there are things that can happen and things that can't. And I'm not going to worry about the things that can't." I was talking too fast.

"All right. What are the things that *can* happen?" The Grandma Therapist smiled. I used to hate it when she smiled— it made me think she wasn't taking me seriously—but now I understood that it was her way of paying attention.

"Floods." I looked at the plant on the table beside me. "The basement flooding. That happened once. Or breaking your leg. Or getting mugged."

"Those are all things you're willing to concede," the Grandma Therapist said. Then, in case I didn't know what *concede* meant, she added, "You're willing to admit the possibility of those things existing."

"Yeah." I noticed that both of my hands were clutching the arms of the chair.

"You aren't looking at me," the Grandma Therapist said. "Is there a reason why?"

"No."

"All right. What are the things that *can't* happen?"

I still couldn't look at her. I was holding a number of invisible doors closed, and it took a lot of concentration. "Things get messed up sometimes," I said. "But then they get better. They don't just get worse and worse and worse. That isn't what happens."

"You want things to make sense. You want a reasonable pattern. Is that what you're saying?"

I didn't answer. I knew I wouldn't be able to explain it, but I used to have a feeling of a promise made to me—a kind of unbreakable, unassailable bargain with the universe: nothing terrible would ever happen to me or my sister. Now I wondered where that feeling had come from. *I want that magic wand after all,* I wanted to say. *And I want a story with a happy ending.*

"Elena?"

"Could Dora have *you* as a therapist?" I asked. I was thinking out loud. Of course I would have to convince Dora that the Grandma Therapist would be worth her while; at first, partly to try to cheer my sister up, I had made fun of the Grandma Therapist and pretended that she was a hundred and eight years old.

"No. I'm not a psychiatrist. Your sister needs more care than I can offer her. And I can't prescribe medication."

I nodded, then pulled a piece of fuzz off the cushion beside me. "Dora's pills have a black box."

"I'm sorry?"

"On the label," I said. I explained that Jimmy had helped me look up my sister's prescriptions, and that at first I had thought, when he said "black box," that he was referring to the devices on airplanes. "Because whenever you hear about a plane crash," I said, "you always hear about people running around trying to figure out how the crash happened. And if they find the black box—you know, the recording—sometimes they can hear the pilots talking and then they can understand what happened and why the plane went down. It made me think that if Dora had a black box inside her, someone could find it and open it up. And they could keep her from crashing. That sounds really weird," I said. "Doesn't it?"

"No, not to me."

I plucked a yellow leaf from her plant. "I don't know why I'm talking so much," I said.

"Maybe you have a lot to say. Are you talking to your parents?"

"They're pretty busy." My mother had dropped me off at my appointment; my father was supposed to pick me up in the lobby.

"This is hard for all of you," the Grandma Therapist said. "It's hard for each of you in different ways. Your part may be especially difficult."

It seemed odd to hear her refer to my *part,* as if I had accidentally won a role in some awful play. "My part is to watch over Dora." I plucked another leaf from the plant.

"I'm not sure what you mean."

"Because of the black box," I said. "Someone's supposed to watch out for her. It even said so online."

The Grandma Therapist leaned forward in her chair and held out her hand for the two dead leaves. "Your sister is suffering from an illness," she said. "But she still has choices. And she still has responsibilities—like everyone else." Her voice was soft. "Is there anything you think you ought to tell me?"

I shook my head.

She dropped the dead leaves into the trash. "Of course you want your sister to get better. But she has her work to do and you have yours. Ultimately," she said, "the responsibility for Dora belongs to Dora."

I looked down at the rug.

"A drowning person doesn't rescue herself," I said, because whenever I thought about the game Dora and I had played when we were little, I pictured Dora struggling and drowning.

"Good point." The Grandma Therapist folded her hands. "Which is why it's so important—for your sister and for everyone else—that she learn how to swim."

Some days I was sure Dora was getting better. She did her homework, dressed Mr. Peebles in my mother's underwear, and spent an hour with a friend on the phone.

And then she would plunge.

My parents' moods were tied to Dora's. When she was happy, they were happy. When she was in tears, they were upset. Only when Dora was asleep in her room did they follow each other down to the kitchen to continue the argument that never ended: *This looks like a nice spot for fighting; let's shout over here.*

I thought about leaving them a note with an arrow pointing to the vent above the cabinets: *This is a heating duct. It leads to my bedroom.*

But I didn't do it. Instead, one night I put on my bathrobe and went downstairs and pushed through the swinging door into the kitchen. "What are you guys talking about?" I asked.

"Elena. It's late," my father said.

"Have you been talking about Dora? Is something going on?"

"Nothing's going on." My mother wiped her face with a towel. "Go back to sleep."

"I thought we were all about communication these days," I said. "I thought we were supposed to—"

"Lena, please," my mother said. "Just leave it alone."

But I couldn't leave it alone. "Did you swallow your pills today?" I asked. Dora and I were walking to the bus stop. I'd left the house with two toaster waffles; I handed one to my sister.

"Yup. Every single pill." She took a bite out of the waffle. "I even swallowed the ones that smell bad. That fish oil makes me stink like a tuna. So. Have you been talking to Mom and Dad about me?"

"What do you mean?"

She took another bite of her waffle, then threw the rest like a Frisbee into the neighbors' yard. "You don't have to lie about it," she said.

I saw Jimmy leaning against the fire hydrant near the bus stop.

"I've seen you talking to them," Dora said. "And I don't blame you." She stopped walking. "Your life would be easier if I went back to Lorning."

"Dora, don't say that." I remembered the smell in the halls at Lorning—air freshener and bandages and cafeteria food.

"And all it would take for Mom and Dad to send me back there," Dora went on, "would be for someone to tell them I was spitting out pills or forging notes or falling asleep when I wasn't supposed to. And do you know what's sad?" She turned to face me; her eyes were underlined with dark half-circles. "You would probably be that person. Who else would it be?"

I heard the bus starting up the hill. *Maybe if we keep moving,* I thought—*maybe if we get on the bus and go to school and move through the day, we'll be able to put this moment behind us.*

"I just want you to be okay, Dora," I said. "I just need to know that when you—"

"Stop." She tucked her damp hair into her sweatshirt. "You need to stop hovering. I don't want you checking on me anymore. I don't want you asking me a thousand questions. You're worse than Mom."

Jimmy was waving us toward the bus.

"Do I look all right?" Dora asked.

She was painfully thin. "You look great," I said.

53

"Why are we having a cookout in November?" I asked Jimmy. "It's freezing out here." It was Saturday afternoon and we were in his backyard. The yard was fenced, and the fence was covered with some kind of ivy.

"This is the best time of year for outdoor grilling." Jimmy dragged a metal fire pit away from the house and started filling it with sticks. "In the summer we'd be too hot sitting around a fire. It'll be even better out here in January." He took a pack of matches from his pocket, crumpled some newspaper in with the twigs, and lit it. "How are you doing? Seventy-five percent water? Eighty percent? What are you thinking?"

I watched the fire grow bigger.

"I don't know. Maybe my brain is fried," I said. "I can barely think straight anymore."

Jimmy unfolded two folding chairs. "Do you want something sweet? Something in the marshmallow family? Or how about veggies—maybe a tuber?"

"I'm not going to stay very long," I said. "Dora's been at Kate's all day, but she's coming home at five-thirty."

We sat down. Jimmy poked the fire with a stick.

"You shouldn't put your life on hold for her," he said.

"Who says I'm putting my life on hold?"

The wind shifted, blowing the smoke toward us. "You don't talk about anything else," he said. "You only talk about your sister."

"She asked me to save her," I said.

Jimmy snapped some twigs and tossed them into the fire. "She shouldn't have."

"Why not?"

"Because it's not fair." He looked annoyed. "And because you can't do it. Are you sure you don't want my mom to talk to your parents?"

"Yeah. I'm sure."

We watched the flames for a while.

Maybe it was the ivy-covered fence or the smell of burnt wood, or maybe it was the scar that made the corner of his mouth uneven. But something persuaded me to kiss Jimmy Zenk. I leaned forward and kissed him. His lips were soft.

Jimmy nodded as if to himself and then backed away slowly. "I don't think this is a very good time for that," he said.

"Oh."

"No offense," he said. "But right now you're upset and we've been talking about your sister. I don't want to make out with you for that reason."

"I didn't kiss you because I'm upset, Jimmy," I said. "I didn't kiss you because of Dora."

"We were just talking about her," he said.

"I know that. I was here, remember?"

"Yeah." Jimmy paused. "I'm just saying it felt inappropriate."

I stood up; my chair collapsed on the ground behind me. "Do you want me to sign a contract before I kiss you? Do you have a list of reasons why kissing is appropriate?"

"Yeah, kind of." He rubbed his hand across the top of his head. "I guess I have a kind of list. But it's not written down or anything."

I walked toward the gate, then turned around. Jimmy was still sitting by the fire. "You always ask me about Dora," I said. "You're the one who told me about Lorning. And you told me to find out about the drugs. You told me to watch her."

"I didn't say *you* should watch her."

I wanted to push him into the fire. "You said I shouldn't put my life on hold. But now you're letting Dora put it on hold. You're letting her take something away from me."

"Nobody's taking me," Jimmy said. "I'll be right here."

54

That night I dreamed I found a box. I picked it up and heard something shuffling and knocking inside it. I knew it was Dora, even though the box was much too small. I lifted it and carefully turned the box over but it was seamless and smooth; there was no opening.

I sat up in bed, my heart thumping away inside my chest.

When I was little and woke up from a nightmare, I used to hurry down the hall to Dora's room. My feet knew the path even in complete darkness: five steps from my bed to the door, and then I could hold out both hands to touch the bumps in the wallpaper and in eight more steps arrive at the safety of my sister's room.

Now that I was older, it was only six steps.

"Dora?" I climbed onto the mattress and lay down next to her. "Are you awake?" I leaned my head against her bony arm.

"Nn," she said. A half-reply.

I wondered what she was dreaming about, if she was dreaming. Downstairs, I could hear my parents in the kitchen. But they didn't seem to be arguing this time. It was harder to hear them from Dora's room.

"Remember when we used to build forts in Mom and Dad's bedroom?" I asked. "We'd use all the blankets and all the pillows, and we'd crawl around on the floor and pretend to get lost?"

"Yeah, I remember."

"That was fun," I said.

"Uh-huh."

"We used to do a lot of that stuff." I wondered if she had fallen back to sleep. "I tried to kiss Jimmy today," I said.

"Ew?" Dora turned over so she was facing me. In the dark she looked different. Her face had changed; it was full of shadows. "What do you mean, 'tried to'?"

"I don't know. He didn't want to do it," I said. "He wouldn't kiss me back. I think I probably did it wrong."

"Maybe you should practice," Dora said. "I used to practice on my hand. Like this." She made a fist and held it toward me in the dark. "My hand used to like it," she said. "No complaints, anyway." She lifted her head off the pillow. "Do you need me to kick Jimmy's ass for you?"

"No," I said. "Thanks."

"Because I'm willing to," Dora said. "I would do it for you."

I could hear our parents coming upstairs. "I wish you had told me when it started, Dora."

She lay back down.

I pulled a strand of her hair from my mouth. Our faces were inches apart on the pillow.

"You used to tell me things," I said. "We used to talk. I wish you had told me." I picked up her skinny arm and draped it over my shoulder. "Everything's going to be okay," I said. "We can still trust each other."

Dora's feet were as cold as ice. The bed was too small for two people, but she didn't tell me to leave and go back to my room.

Dora's friends Kate and Lila sat down next to me in the cafeteria. "We came to talk to you," Kate said. "To the little sister." She sipped from a plastic water bottle.

"Can I have your carrot sticks?" Lila asked.

I handed them over. There was an awkward silence.

"Maybe it's nothing," Lila said. "But did Dora get in trouble last weekend?"

"For what?" I asked.

Kate took another swig of her water. "She said she was grounded."

"She wasn't grounded." I threw the rest of my lunch away. "She was with you guys." I looked at Kate. "She was at your house on Saturday."

Kate twisted the lid back onto her bottle of water. "I don't know whose house she was at," she said. "But it wasn't mine."

On my way back to class I left a sticky note on Dora's locker. *Fqkpi mi? Doing ok?*

On my own locker, an hour later, I found her answer: *Uvqr uyrafgle og.*

Stop watching me.

"You're particularly quiet today," the Grandma Therapist said.

I sagged down in her chair. I liked her chair; there were all different ways a person could sit in it.

"Are you getting enough sleep?"

I didn't answer.

"We'll need to talk about that," she said. "But what have you been thinking about and feeling this past week?" She waited. She seemed to have the ability to wait forever. Wasn't she concerned that my parents were paying for these empty minutes?

I thought about the different things I could tell her: that I had tried to kiss Jimmy, that my parents barely noticed me anymore, that our lives at home revolved around making sure Dora took her pills and went to school, and that we gauged her mood almost every minute of every day.

"I like your office," I said.

"Thank you." The Grandma Therapist nodded. "What else are you thinking?"

"I'm not sure yet." I felt a few invisible doors begin to open, as if someone were tugging at my skin. "Sometimes I wonder," I said.

"What do you wonder?"

The room was so quiet I could hear the ticking of the clock.

"Sometimes when I think about Dora I wonder, you

know—" I felt my pulse beating in my throat. "I wonder what I'm supposed to *do* with it." I looked around her office—the lamp, the rug, the bookshelf, the table with the box of tissues and the jar of stones—and I felt as if I were waiting for the end of a story, for the moment when the crisis passed and the characters wisely understood what had happened to them and someone shut the book with a satisfying snap. But what if the story didn't end, and the book stayed open?

"You wonder what you're supposed to do with what?" the Grandma Therapist asked.

"This." I couldn't look at her. I tried to gesture but ended up just turning my hands palm up in my lap. *This thing,* I wanted to say to her. *This giant shape always pressing and bruising and taking up every single particle of air between us.*

The Grandma Therapist leaned toward me. "Are you talking about sadness?"

I could barely speak above a whisper. "I don't know what I'm supposed to do with it," I said. "What do other people do with it? Where do they put it?"

She didn't answer right away. "Sometimes they carry it with them," she said. "Because they aren't sure what else to do."

I nodded.

"But sometimes they open it up like a package in the presence of a person they can talk to," she said. "Someone they can trust." She held out her hands. "Any person who is carrying a lot of sadness," she said, "needs to be able to rest sometimes, and to put it down."

58

"So I wasn't sure you'd want to see me," Jimmy said when I answered the door and found him standing on the porch. "But I figured you'd be home and I got inspired, so I brought you this." He held out a plastic food container and took off the lid.

"That's kind of a weird-looking snack," I said.

"Actually, it's incredible." Jimmy didn't wait to be invited; he came right into the house and followed me to the study. Dora and my mother were out somewhere, so we were alone. "It's basically chickpeas and feta cheese and mint," he said. "This stuff is nutritious. It's got protein, and something else. I forget what. Dairy or something. If you ever decide to be a vegetarian you could practically live on it."

"I'm not a vegetarian."

"Why don't you get us some bowls and some spoons?" Jimmy sat down. When I came back, I found him engrossed in a commercial for tampons. I had to wave the spoons in front of him. "Jimmy?"

"What? Sorry: I don't usually watch TV," he said. "You know the average kid watches a thousand hours during the school year?" He dished out the salad. "So how's she doing?"

I ate a couple of chickpeas, carefully dragging the chunks of feta to the edge of the bowl. "She's doing okay."

"She doesn't look it," Jimmy said. "If you want my opinion."

"I don't want your opinion. And I don't want to argue about it," I said.

"Who's arguing?" A few flecks of mint colored the corners of his mouth. "Actually, I came over because I wanted to talk to you."

"Surprise," I said. "We're already talking."

"Yeah. Here's what I'm thinking, though," Jimmy said. "I'm thinking that maybe this situation is getting beyond you."

"Just leave it alone, Jimmy," I said.

He ate a spoonful of salad. "You don't know what she might be involved in."

"She's not 'involved in' anything." I picked up the remote and changed the channel. "Last time you criticized me for always talking about Dora. And now here you are, talking about her again."

"Here I am," Jimmy agreed.

We stared at the TV for a while. "You know what I've noticed about you?" I asked. "You never say you're sorry about my sister. That's what other people say. Either they pretend they don't know anything or they say, 'I'm sorry to hear about your sister.' But you never say that."

"Do you want me to say it?"

"No."

Jimmy put the lid on his plastic container. "I'm going upstairs."

"What for?" I got up and followed him. "You're not going to shave your head again, are you?"

"No. But I shaved my chin yesterday." He turned around at the foot of the stairs with his hand on the banister. "Do you want to feel it?"

"I'll pass."

He took the steps two at a time. My parents' bedroom door was open; Jimmy walked in. The room was neat. The bed was made and each of the dressers had only a few simple things on its surface: a wooden tray for my father, and for my mother, a jewelry box, a jar of lotion, and a brush and comb. Jimmy picked up a stack of books on the bedside table. *Your Depressed Adolescent. A Guide to Psychiatric Drugs. Your Difficult Teen.* "Good reading," he said. He tested the mattress with his hand. "Firm. That's good for your back. Which one is your room?"

"I don't want you in my bedroom, Jimmy."

He paused at the laundry chute, opened it, and peered inside. "Then where *do* you want me? Just kidding." He walked down the hall, paused briefly at the doorway of my room, and kept on walking. "This is Dora's room, right? I'm good at guessing."

"You had a fifty-fifty chance. Where are you going?" I followed him into my sister's room. About a year earlier Dora had painted the walls a deep purple; even with the light on, the room was gloomy. "We're not allowed to have guys upstairs, Jimmy."

"Does she keep a diary?" he asked.

Dora's desk was about fourteen inches deep in paper. "I wouldn't read it if she did," I said.

Jimmy ran a hand over the bristles on his head and looked around. The room was crowded with stuff, the bed and the floor piled deep with clothes. Over the bed Dora had hung her favorite poster—a picture of the Eiffel Tower at night, frayed at the bottom from being touched. On the other walls were a row of beaded purses she had collected from various thrift stores; a clock in the shape of a cat, the eyes moving back and forth in time with its rhinestone tail; a Tinker Bell mirror on which Tinker Bell's clothes had all been painted black with indelible marker; and a lamp with a dented shade on which Dora had written in purple nail polish DORA ROCKS.

Jimmy waded through the piles of clothes to the dresser, then picked up the metal box where Dora kept her jewelry.

"What are you doing?" I asked.

He looked in the box, closed it, and put it back down. He took the plug out of Dora's piggy bank and stuck his finger inside, then opened a plastic container full of makeup, spilling half of it onto the floor. He opened her sock drawer and rifled through it, then opened the drawer where she kept her brightly colored bras.

"Jimmy, stop."

He ignored me, combing through the rest of Dora's drawers; he opened her closet and poked through her bookshelf. He picked her shoes up and shook them, and lifted the pillows on her bed.

"You're being a jerk, Jimmy," I said. "I really hate you right now."

He saw me glance at the clock with the cat's tail ticking away underneath it. He gently lifted the clock from the wall and turned it over. Taped to the inside was a plastic bag.

"What is that?" I asked.

Jimmy held the bag open: inside it were about a hundred little white pills.

I held out my hand, even though I didn't want to touch what he was holding.

"I'm sorry about your sister," Jimmy said.

When Dora and my mother got home (Jimmy had already gone), Dora announced that she was starving and was going to make grilled cheese for dinner. And I was going to help her with her homework while she cooked.

"That sounds good to me." My mother looked cheerful. She got out the electric griddle and a can of soup.

Dora slapped her open history book on the table and pointed to a paragraph in the middle of a chapter. "Here you go, Elvin. Have a seat and start reading. I've got to get me an education."

I sat down. I had the bag of pills in my pocket.

"What's the matter?" Dora asked.

"Nothing."

My mother got out the broom, humming to herself.

I started to read. " 'The colonialists were welcome at first,' " I read, " 'but resentment and conflict set in quickly.' "

"Yeah, obvious," Dora said. She lined up a dozen pieces of bread beside the stove and dumped the soup into a pot. "Wait, what country are they talking about?"

"I don't know." I flipped through the chapter. I was having trouble concentrating. "India, I think. Or maybe it's Africa."

"Okay, whatever. Same story." She turned on the griddle. My mother swept the floor around her.

" 'When disagreements over land use arose—' "

"You're reading too slow. Skip to the stuff in the box,"

Dora said. "They always have a box at the end of the chapter where they summarize things. Should I use cheddar or Swiss?"

"Swiss." I flipped to the end of the chapter but didn't see a box.

My father came home from work, wandered into the kitchen, and smacked his forehead with his hand when he saw Dora at the stove. He said, "Man alive, that looks good. Will there be enough for me?"

"Only if you'll stop being corny and saying things like 'man alive,' " Dora told him.

"Deal." My father picked up a spatula and started chasing Dora with it. My mother asked them to stop acting like pirates.

"Pirates!" Dora laughed so hard I thought she'd be sick.

"Look, snow," my father said, pointing out the window with his spatula. "The first snow of the year. It almost never snows this early. Now, that's something."

I wished Jimmy could see us.

After we ate, my parents went for a walk and left Dora and me to do the dishes.

"So. What's going on with you?" Dora asked.

We stood at the sink side by side, our hands dipping into the soapy water. I found myself wishing we were younger. I wished we were putting on our boots by the back door and getting ready to go outside and play.

"I found your pills," I said.

Dora's hands paused for a few seconds, her bracelets making a quiet music.

"The ones you hid behind the clock. I thought I should tell you."

She turned to face me. "You must hate this so much."

"It's okay," I said.

"No, it isn't." She wiped some soapsuds off my wrist. "Did you look at the pills?"

I didn't answer.

"I don't want them back. I just want you to look at them before you flush them down the toilet. They're for cramps, Lay-Lay. You know how bad my cramps can get."

I rinsed off a handful of silverware.

"I bought a bottle at the drugstore," Dora said. "I knew Mom wouldn't let me have them, so I hid them away."

Through the kitchen window I could see that the snow was still falling; the world was gradually turning white.

"I know what you're thinking," Dora said. "But look: I'm standing here talking to you, right? And I don't want the pills. You can have them." She looked out the window. "If you tell Mom and Dad, they'll probably tell Dr. Siebald, and if there's an open bed at Lorning—"

I held up my hand; I had to make her stop talking. "I need you to promise me something," I said.

Dora plunged a greasy platter into the sink. "I think you just aged about twenty years," she muttered. "You sound like Mom."

"I mean it," I said. "I need you to promise that if you ever feel bad—I mean, as bad as you did when—"

Dora whirled toward me, grinning, and slung a wet and soapy arm around my neck. She crooked her elbow to pull me close so we were knee to knee, rib cage to rib cage, forehead to forehead. "Sweetheart," she said, in a perfect imitation of our mother's voice. "If there's ever anything you need to tell me, anything at all . . ."

"Dora, I'm not kidding." I tried to push her away, but she held onto me tightly. Her eyeballs were about an inch away from mine. The soap from her hand was dripping down my shirt.

"You have to promise that you'll come and find me. Promise," I said. "If you feel really bad, you'll come and tell me. I need you to promise."

"Your breath smells like cheese," Dora said.

But I wouldn't stop nagging until she promised.

60

On the bus on the way to school the next morning, Dora insisted on sitting next to me. She told me a series of knock-knock jokes that weren't funny, but we laughed anyway.

In Mr. Clearwater's class that afternoon (everyone was roaming from desk to desk, because the bell hadn't rung yet), Jimmy asked me what I'd done with the pills.

"Threw them out." I hadn't tried to find out what they were; I had gone out the night before and dumped them into a neighbor's trash can.

"What are those marks for?" he asked.

While we'd been talking I had uncapped a marker and added to the long row of check marks on the inside of my backpack.

"It's just something I do." I counted the marks: forty-eight days since Dora had been admitted to Lorning.

He leaned over my shoulder. "Thanksgiving is only two weeks away, if you're counting something."

I had almost forgotten about Thanksgiving.

Jimmy obviously hadn't. He said his mother was going to let him make most of the meal. He was going to put oysters in the stuffing. He was going to make cranberry relish with apricots in it. He was going to invent a pecan pie the likes of which no one in the world had seen before.

"You told your parents, right?" he asked. "About the pills?"

The bell rang. Mr. Clearwater clapped his hands at the

front of the room, straightened his mustache, and started droning on about the American Revolution.

Ten minutes later there was a knock at the door—a student runner from the main office. "Oh, hey, sorry for the interruption and all that." The student had blond hair and looked like a surfer. He waved a slip of paper in Mr. Clearwater's direction. "For Elena Lindt. She's supposed to go to the main office. Right away, chop-chop."

Everybody started up with the usual comments about how I probably got caught selling drugs on the Internet or setting fire to a police car.

I collected my books. Jimmy got halfway out of his chair and touched my elbow.

"What?" I asked.

He didn't say anything.

A bottle of pills, a tube of glue: she broke her promise.

A woman in a minivan stopped when she saw her. Dora had been sitting with her praying-mantis legs folded underneath her, under the overpass a quarter mile from school. "She just didn't look right," the woman said. The woman—I never knew her name but I listened in on the extension when she talked to my parents that night—saw Dora sitting under the overpass in the middle of a school day and decided to pull over to the side of the road, a very kind thing for a stranger to do. "I saw her and I wondered and I almost kept driving," the woman said, "and then I thought, *She looks so young!* What if that was my child and no one stopped? I wouldn't have been able to live with myself."

The woman parked fifty yards down the road and got out of her minivan and walked back into the shade of the overpass, where my sister was crumpled up on the pavement by herself in the cold. The woman leaned over Dora and asked her if she was all right.

"No," Dora said.

"Do you need help, honey?" the woman asked.

"No," Dora said. But the woman helped her anyway.

In a private waiting room at the hospital, my mother was shaking. Her hands, her arms, her whole body was shaking. "She walked right out of school and no one stopped her?" my mother asked. She put on her I-am-so-amazed face, like one of those masks you see in a theater. My father and I were her only audience. "Do they just let their students wander in and out of the building? How long had she been missing class? And no one called us? They just allowed my daughter to walk away?"

"Gail, stop," my father said. "This isn't helping."

"Don't touch me," my mother said. She turned fiercely, abruptly to me. "You knew she was cutting class, didn't you?"

I didn't need to give her an answer. I could tell by the look on her face that, in some corner of her mind, I might as well have given my sister the collection of pills and the tube of glue and then opened the front door of the school and ushered her out. *Off you go, Dora. Best of luck.*

"But you didn't tell us," my mother said. "You decided to keep that information to yourself."

"Gail, please," my father said.

My mother ignored him. She was still shaking. Her watch loosened itself from her wrist, the watch face sliding along her arm. "What else did you decide not to tell us?" *She wants to hit me,* I thought, *but she's never done it before so she doesn't know how.* I wished she would hit me. "You put your sister's life in danger. She might have died."

"Gail." My father was crying. I had never seen my father cry.

"What did she tell you?" My mother was shouting, but for some reason I could barely hear her. "What did she tell you? What did you know?"

64

Here is what I knew, or thought I knew:

(1) Dora would never break a promise—at least, not a promise she had made to me.
(2) My parents weren't interested in what I thought.
(3) I could learn how to open the black box, I could do it myself; it was up to me.

What would I have done if Dora had confided in me? If she had found me in the hall between classes and slung her arm around my neck so that we were eyeball to eyeball and said, *Hey, Lena, instead of going to class next period I'm going to leave the building and I am going to poison myself and sit under the overpass and maybe you will never see me again?*

I would have called our parents.

And they would have called Dr. Siebald.

Which is what happened anyway. Dora was already back at Lorning.

When Jimmy called later that night (my parents were fighting in the garage instead of the kitchen) I carried the phone into my room and shut the door. I lay down on the carpet and looked at the specks of dust that could only be seen from that angle.

"She's at Lorning again," I said.

I could hear Jimmy breathing.

"She could have had brain damage," I told him. "From the glue and the pills. But they told us she doesn't."

"That's good," Jimmy said. "So how are *you* doing?"

I pulled a thread out of the carpet.

"I could just stay on the phone with you, if you want," Jimmy said. "If it would help."

I didn't answer.

"We don't have to talk or anything. I'll be right here and you can talk if you want to. Or not. You can just hold the phone."

I held on to the phone.

"I can talk or be quiet," Jimmy said. "Either one. Not talking is hard, but I'll do my best. I'll start right now. Ready?"

I fell asleep with Jimmy's silence held to my ear.

I didn't go to school the next day. I got up late and took a long bath, ate part of an ice cream bar for breakfast, and ended up taking a nap on a pile of clothes in Dora's room.

My father woke me up at six-thirty that evening. "You've been sleeping all day," he said. "Your mother and I are going to the hospital. Do you want to come?"

I pushed a pile of Dora's shirts off the edge of the mattress. "Fridays aren't visiting days," I said.

"That doesn't matter anymore. We talked to the nurses." My father held out his hand and helped me up.

"Do you and Mom hate me?"

"No. We could never hate you."

I leaned against him. He had an ink stain on his pocket. "I wanted to talk to you," I said. "I tried."

"I know." My father tugged on my hair. "We weren't listening."

My parents had to fill out some paperwork at the nurses' station, which meant that Dora and I were in the conference room alone. Dora was wearing a T-shirt over hospital pajamas. The other kids—I had expected them to look familiar but of course they didn't—were already getting ready for bed.

"You look tired. Actually, you look like crap," Dora said.

"You look like crap too."

"Yeah, but I was better-looking to start with." She pulled her feet up onto her chair and hugged her legs. "You think I've ruined everything, don't you?"

"No. But I don't understand what happened," I said. "I thought—"

"The food here is even worse than last time," Dora said. "It's incredible what they try to get us to eat." She put her head on her knees.

I looked out the conference room door; my parents were still standing at the nurses' station. "When you get home this time," I said, "maybe we can sleep in the same room the way we used to. We can use my room for a place to hang out and listen to music, and—"

"I'm not going to come home," Dora mumbled.

"What do you mean?"

She lifted her head and shook out her hair. "I'm too much of a risk. Does that sound familiar?"

"No," I said.

"Whatever. Don't worry about it. It'll be easier for you at school if I'm not around. That was a part of the decision."

"What decision?" I asked.

My parents seemed to be finishing up. My father was clutching a thick batch of papers.

"You searched my room," Dora said.

Out in the hall, someone started to cry.

"I didn't tell them, Dora," I said. I lowered my voice. "I didn't tell Mom and Dad."

"Well, somebody told them." She sat back and looked at me, then nibbled the tangled ends of her hair. "Have you kissed him yet?"

The day seemed to be speeding up without me, leaving me behind. "You have to come home, Dora," I said. "Where else would you go?"

"Ask Jimmy." She almost smiled. "Now you can start to forget all about me. Poof!" She waved her skinny arms in the air. "I'm already gone."

I barely spoke to my parents on the way home. And as soon as I walked in the door I dialed Jimmy's number and told him I was coming over to talk to him.

"When?" he asked. "Lena? I was just getting ready to—"

"Now," I said. "I'm coming over right now."

"Wow, that was fast," Jimmy said when he opened the door.

I put my hands in my pockets—not because I was cold, but because I thought I might have to hit him. "You told my parents about the pills."

"I had to." He nodded. "I told my mom."

I felt as if I'd been robbed. As if someone had broken into my life and ignored all the things that a person should steal—my CD player and my wallet and the silver earrings my parents had given me—and took the only thing that mattered, the thing I didn't understand could be stolen.

Jimmy touched my arm. "Do you want to come in?"

"They're going to send her away," I said. Eighty-two percent water.

"Jimmy, is the door open?" a voice asked.

"Yeah, it's okay, Mom," Jimmy said. "I'll be right back." He came outside and shut the door behind him. The porch light above us turned his face yellow.

"They're going to send her to a treatment center. Does that sound familiar?" I took my hands out of my pockets and grabbed his wrists.

"You have to let it go," Jimmy said. Or maybe he said, "You have to let her go."

I wasn't letting anything go. "Am I hurting you?"

"Yes."

I squeezed even harder. My fingers ached, I was squeezing so hard. Then, under my left middle finger, on Jimmy's wrist, I felt a line—a series of lines like small seams in his skin. I remembered him warning me about Dora cutting herself.

I turned his arms over. "You don't have a brother," I said.

"I do."

"But he wasn't at Lorning. You were at Lorning." I pulled up his sleeve and saw the lines on his forearm; by the yellow light on the porch ceiling I saw dozens of scars crosshatching his skin from his wrist to his elbow.

"All this time." I let go of his arms. "That's how you knew about Lorning. And about the doctors and the drugs. And you didn't tell me."

"I wanted to," Jimmy said. "I was—"

But I cut him off. "I told you everything about Dora. And you've been making up a story about your brother. You lied to me, Jimmy."

"Yeah," Jimmy said. "I guess I did."

I told my parents I didn't want to talk. There was no reason to sit down for a pointless discussion, because everything was already finished and decided. There was nothing to say.

"Lena, just listen to us for a minute," my father said. "Lorning isn't suited to what Dora's been going through. She needs more time in a different environment."

I found one of Dora's empty pill bottles behind the toaster. I picked it up.

"None of us wanted this to happen," my mother said. "But Marilyn Zenk had some very good recommendations, and your father and I found a place in New Hampshire—"

"I have to clean my room. And I have homework," I said.

My father pointed out that it was Saturday. "You never do homework on Saturdays."

"Big project," I said. I put on my earphones and went up to my room.

Several hours later my mother knocked at my door and said Jimmy was downstairs waiting to see me.

"Busy," I said.

So he left me a note. *"I an apologiying."* He'd tried to write it in code.

Even when she asked for me specifically, that night and also the next afternoon, I refused to talk to Dora on the phone.

Eighty-eight percent water.

"So you're determined not to talk to her or see her before she leaves," the Grandma Therapist said. We were meeting on Monday instead of Tuesday. My mother had taken me out of school for an "emergency appointment." "Do you think you might regret that decision?"

I didn't answer. The Grandma Therapist was having to talk more than she usually did.

"Your parents aren't blaming you for what happened," she said. "But they feel you should have told them about your sister's behavior. And of course you should have, though it would have been difficult. Lena? Are you with me?"

I had a strange feeling inside my chest. I had to sit still and listen for it.

"Last time you were here," the Grandma Therapist went on, "we talked about whether you were feeling sad. I wonder if we should leave that aside for a while, because it occurs to me that you're angry, too. Do you think you're angry?"

I put a hand on my rib cage. Maybe one of my lungs had deflated.

"You might feel angry at your friend and at his mother." She tilted her head. "And you might feel angry at your parents. And also at Dora."

Ninety-one percent water.

"You might feel disappointed as well," the Grandma Therapist said. "Is it possible you're disappointed with yourself?"

"We want you to go with us," my mother said. "We feel very strongly that you should come. You'll only miss two days of school."

"I already missed half a day today," I said. "Besides, I have a Spanish test. I have to bring up my A-minus."

My mother lightly touched a finger to the bridge of her nose. "Lena," she said. Her eyes were bloodshot. "This is all very hard. And you probably think we've been ignoring you. And maybe we have. But you aren't the only one who's been suffering."

"I'm all right," I said. "You don't have a reason to worry about me."

My father said he didn't want me to sleep at the house alone.

"I'll stay with the Fentons." The Fentons lived diagonally behind us; Dora and I babysat their kids.

"But Dora wants to see you," my mother said.

I told her I'd already talked to Mrs. Fenton. It was all set up. It was too late to cancel.

My mother looked disappointed. "Then come to the hospital with us tonight. You can say goodbye to Dora then."

I said I'd write her a note.

But I didn't write one. And I let my parents go to the hospital alone.

My parents were supposed to pick Dora up at the hospital on Tuesday morning after breakfast (my mother had packed Dora's suitcase the night before) and start driving to New Hampshire by eleven o'clock.

But when I got off the bus after school at 3:15, I saw my father's car parked at the side of the road. My father was in the driver's seat (he was leaning back as if asleep) with my mother beside him. Dora was in back. She watched me walk toward her. Then she rolled down the window. "Hey," she said.

She had washed her hair. That was the first thing I noticed. Her hair was so pretty.

"Why are you standing so far away over there?" she asked. "I've been waiting to see you."

I walked toward the car. I put my hands on the backseat window. Dora had rolled it halfway down.

"I didn't want to leave without saying goodbye to you," she said.

I was gripping the window.

"Miss you already." She put both her hands on top of mine. "Don't borrow my stuff."

"I'm sorry, Dora," I said, but my voice was so soft, she probably didn't hear it.

"Don't stay mad at Jimmy," she said. "Kiss him if you want to."

Ninety-three percent water.

"I don't want to be here without you," I said.

Dora opened the car door, nearly knocking me over. She stood up. I had looked up into her face since the day I was born.

"Don't go," I said. "Please."

"I have to," Dora said. "It's the first right thing."

And then she hugged me, and pressed a note into my hand, and left.

Love you, Dora had written.

Cu ʒge cu rfc uma. As big as the sky.

I slept in the Fentons' guest room that night, my face pressed to a lumpy sofa cushion because no one had remembered to give me a pillow. In the morning I got up late and only had time to throw on my clothes, grab my backpack and my jacket, and race out the door. I cut through the Fentons' side yard, then ran up the street to my own front door, taking the key out of my pocket and walking in.

The house was quiet. I stood in the hall for a minute and listened.

I thought about writing Dora a letter but no one had given me her address.

The doorbell rang. I jumped: maybe the Fentons had driven by and noticed that I wasn't at the bus stop. I would have to tell them I had forgotten something. I had forgotten a book I needed at school.

I went to the door and carefully pulled back the curtain: Jimmy.

"Go away," I said. I dropped the curtain.

He rang again.

Because I didn't want anyone seeing him, and because I knew he was capable of standing there for hours, I opened the door.

"You missed the bus," he said, pointing behind him toward the main road. "It just pulled away. And you're usually so good about getting to school. Prompt, and all that. So I came by to see if you were sick."

I straightened the curtain. "You don't need to be here. We don't need to talk or anything."

"Huh," Jimmy said.

"Anyway, I'm not allowed to have guys in the house when my parents are gone, so you'll have to leave."

"Yeah. No guys in the house is a good rule. Responsible parenting and all that." He didn't leave. "The thing is, I bet you didn't eat much this morning, and I didn't either, so I'm going to need to make us some breakfast." He was stamping his feet because of the cold. "And your house is the easiest place to do that, since we're both here already. You know, a good breakfast is the most important part of your day."

We stared at each other for a minute.

"I'm not making that up," Jimmy said. "It's true. Scientific fact."

"Fine," I said. And I let him in.

77

Jimmy made eggs with red peppers and canned corn and cheese, and he stuffed the whole mess inside two pieces of pita bread smeared with mayonnaise. Then, even though my share of the mess looked disgusting, he told me to eat it. I did.

"I should have told you about Lorning," he said while we ate. "I tried to tell you a couple of months ago, but you thought I was talking about my brother. Do you want more eggs?"

I shook my head.

"I was there for two months," Jimmy said. "I missed the end of ninth grade and most of the summer."

"I wouldn't have told anyone," I said.

"You probably wouldn't have," Jimmy agreed. "But I didn't know that. I mean, at first."

We finished eating. I cleared the dishes.

"You seem pretty calm," Jimmy said. "Are you doing okay?"

I nodded.

"It's good that you saw her before she left." He handed me the pan from the stove. "One day at a time is a good motto. People recover. You want to keep that in mind. Look how well adjusted I usually manage to seem."

I finished the dishes and went into the bathroom to brush my hair, and when I came back Jimmy was hanging up the phone.

"I wanted to tell my mom where I was," he said. "In case the school calls. I didn't want her to worry."

"You told your mother you were cutting school and making breakfast at my house?"

"Yeah. What should I have told her?"

"I don't know," I said.

"She told me we should take the city bus to school." Jimmy ran a hand over his hair. It was growing out and looked almost normal. "We'll just miss the first hour. Do you have any change?"

I opened the junk drawer in the kitchen where my mother usually kept a roll of quarters. Right next to the quarters was a picture of Dora and me. Jimmy looked at it over my shoulder. "Cute," he said. "You should talk to your parents. They're worried about you. That's what I think."

I counted out some quarters and closed the drawer.

We left the house.

"I have a confession," Jimmy said as we walked down the street. "I also didn't tell you I was at Lorning because I thought you might not want to hang out with me if you knew." The air was cold—about twenty degrees—and his breath was turning into frosted clouds above us.

"Do you have any other confessions?" I asked.

"Yeah." He reached into his pocket and offered me something square and yellow. "Candy?"

I squinted. "Is it clean?"

"Not really."

I ate it anyway. "What's your other confession?"

We turned the corner and headed for the main road. "I feel bad I didn't kiss you," Jimmy said. "That day in my yard."

"Oh."

"And I'm kind of wondering if we could try it again."

I glanced at the scar on his upper lip. "I'll think it over."

"Good." Jimmy nodded. "Great." He put his hand on my arm. "When?"

The city bus let us off at an intersection; we still had to walk about half a mile.

"I'll bet it's pretty up there in New Hampshire," Jimmy said. "Woods and mountains and snow and stuff. A lot of nature."

The school was a gray box in the distance.

"My mom had a treatment center picked out for me in Maine, but in the end, I didn't need it. Maine's probably a lot like New Hampshire except for the ocean."

I moved my backpack to my other shoulder.

"Are you getting tired?" Jimmy asked.

When we were little, Dora had helped me attach playing cards to the spokes of my bike wheels. She had showed me how to slice bananas the long way. I had learned to walk by holding on to the back of her dress.

"I only ask because you're slowing down a lot. We could take a rest."

Ninety-five percent water.

"The important thing," Jimmy said, "is that you always stood by her. You couldn't fix everything for her, and you couldn't see inside her head, but she knows you love her. Right? You're probably already writing her secret messages."

We crossed the road to the median strip, a grassy island in the middle of the four-lane. I stopped and adjusted my backpack again.

"The light's still green." Jimmy pointed. "Should we cross?"

I needed to be closer to the ground.

"Lena?"

Ninety-eight percent water.

I dropped to my knees. Cars drove past in both directions.

I thought about what the Grandma Therapist had told me. You learn to carry it with you. But sometimes, in the presence of a person you trust—

"I was supposed to save her, Jimmy," I said. "She asked me to save her."

The traffic streamed by on either side of us.

Ninety-nine percent water.

"I'm right here with you," Jimmy said. He took my backpack, my jacket, my scarf, and my gloves and, kneeling beside me in the frozen grass, he helped me put them down.

author's note

Black Box is a novel, not a true story. I was a liar as a kid and I am a fiction writer by trade and so my impulse in this book, as in each of my other books, was to use the images and ideas and emotions in my head to tell a story. And although *Black Box* is about depression, it is also about family loyalty and honesty and shame and love and denial and about the desire to save someone who is in danger, and who may or may not want to be saved. It is not an account of anyone's real-life experience, but the emotions are as truthful as I could make them.

I started writing *Black Box* because a person very close to me was struggling through some difficult years in the valley of the shadow of depression, which (if you've experienced it, you know) affects not only the sufferer but also the sufferer's loved ones. Like other illnesses—but more so— depression can instill fear and bewilderment and isolation. Unlike other illnesses, depression often comes with an unexpected burden of enormous shame.

The shame is toxic. It can keep people whose very lives are in danger from telling anyone about the danger they're in. (This is akin to standing at the edge of a cliff in the dark and being too ashamed to call out for light.)

It can convince people who suffer from depression that they deserve to suffer or will always suffer.

It can convince people who are in desperate need of human interaction to pretend they don't need to talk to anyone. I know teenagers who were hospitalized for depression but who were instructed to tell their grandparents and teachers that they'd been on vacation. I know people whose family members were hospitalized after suicide attempts but who, when asked how those family members were feeling, always answered "Fine."

"Fine" is not always the correct or appropriate answer. But because we live in a culture of success—and because we tend to measure ourselves by our status as soccer team captains, award-winning pianists, leaders of the youth group, scholarship winners—we often find it difficult, when someone asks "So how are you doing?" to answer anything but "Fine." And our friends and families take note of our shame and are infected by it.

Whenever I drive along the highway and see the billboards about suicide awareness and depression, I take time to look at the faces of the people—most of them are young—who took their own lives. I look at their faces and I think about the suffering they went through (most likely accompanied by an abysmal loneliness) and then I think about their families deciding to display those photos on a highway billboard.

Those families have taken the most painful, the most isolating, the most difficult and potentially shameful thing in their lives and they have blown it up and installed it on the side of a highway so that anyone driving past can see it; they are in effect saying, *This terrible dark thing happened to us, but we don't want to be alone with it anymore, and so we make a gift to you of this picture in the hope that you will see it and recognize*

*it and not be alone and ashamed if something like this, God for-
bid, should ever happen to you.* These are people who have
stopped pretending, and the bravery of those billboards
always brings me to tears.

Black Box was a difficult book for me to write. At least one
person I greatly trust told me that if I needed to write it, fine;
but I should certainly never publish it. I thought about not
publishing it, and I thought about whether I would be a bad
person for wanting to see the book in print.

Ultimately my decision to publish *Black Box* came back to
shame and to isolation. I thought about the people I had met
who were in pain but were pretending that everything was
fine. And I thought, *This is what books can do for us: they can
acknowledge our experience and take the lid off our isolation
and make us feel less alone.* To me, books have always been a
great source of comfort—not because they allow for
escapism (though that's certainly one of their benefits) but
because they offer recognition. Face to face with other people, we might give in to the impulse to pretend that everything is "fine"; but when we open the cover of a book—I'm
talking mostly about novels here—there is no shame and no
need to pretend. Good fiction has never lied to me. When I
immerse myself in a book I feel recognized and therefore
relieved. I turn the pages and think, *Yes, I have felt that too—
that loneliness and joy and anxiety and confusion and fear.*
When I read, what once seemed meaningless gains meaning,
and I am not alone.

That's what I hope for from *Black Box*. I hope I've taken
what felt painful and random and bewildering and, in sifting

it onto the pages of this book, have created meaning. I hope—whether you have experienced depression or not—that you will recognize some part of who you are and feel acknowledged; that you will feel steadied by the imaginative solace a good book can provide.

Depression is treatable.
If you or someone you know is suffering from depression,
ask for help. You aren't alone.
Talk to an adult you can trust, and learn more at
www.helpguide.org/mental/depression_teen_teenagers.htm.

If you are in danger and need help right away,
call the National Suicide Prevention Lifeline at
1-800-273-TALK (8255).

about the author

Julie Schumacher is the author of *The Book of One Hundred Truths,* winner of the Minnesota Book Award for Young Adult Fiction; *The Chain Letter;* and *Grass Angel,* a PEN Center USA Literary Award Finalist for Children's Literature. She is also the author of numerous short stories and two books for adults, including *The Body Is Water,* an Ernest Hemingway Foundation/PEN Award Finalist for First Fiction and an ALA Notable Book of the Year.

Julie Schumacher is the director of the creative writing program and a professor of English at the University of Minnesota. She lives with her family in St. Paul. Visit her at www.julieschumacher.com.